War is Hell.

The air crackled with the heat of powerbolts as they tore through the forest. The skimmers caught the brunt of it and many of them flashed through incandescence into ash. Others were not so lucky, as powerbolts tore through the innards of men and left them brief seconds of shocked horror before they died.

Often the only difference between the victor and the vanquished is that one can smell death and the other smells of death. That was the way of it now . . .

Slammers Down!

The Combat Command Books from Ace:

COMBAT COMMAND: In the world of Piers Anthony's
BIO OF A SPACE TYRANT, CUT BY EMERALD
by Dana Kramer

COMBAT COMMAND: In the world of Robert A. Heinlein's
STARSHIP TROOPERS, SHINES THE NAME
by Mark Acres

COMBAT COMMAND: In the world of Keith Laumer's
STAR COLONY, THE OMEGA REBELLION
by Troy Denning

COMBAT COMMAND: In the world of David Drake's
HAMMER'S SLAMMERS, SLAMMERS DOWN!
by Todd Johnson

COMBAT COMMAND: In the world of Jack Williamson's
THE LEGION OF SPACE, THE LEGION AT WAR
by Andrew Keith
(coming in April)

COMBAT COMMAND™

IN THE WORLD OF

DAVID DRAKE'S HAMMER'S SLAMMERS

SLAMMERS DOWN!

BY
TODD JOHNSON

WITH AN AFTERWORD BY
DAVID DRAKE

ACE BOOKS, NEW YORK

This book is an Ace original edition,
and has never been previously published.

SLAMMERS DOWN!

An Ace Book / published by arrangement with
Bill Fawcett & Associates

PRINTING HISTORY
Ace edition / Feburary 1988

To Anne McCaffrey—of course!

REGARRA

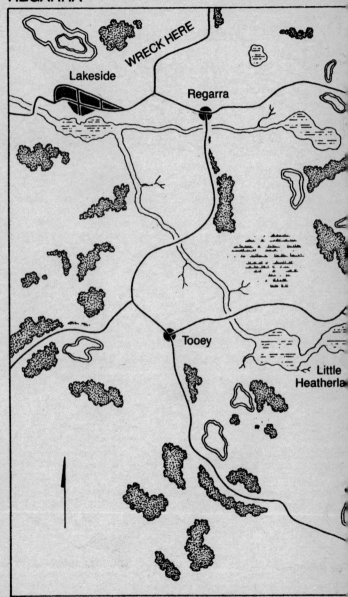

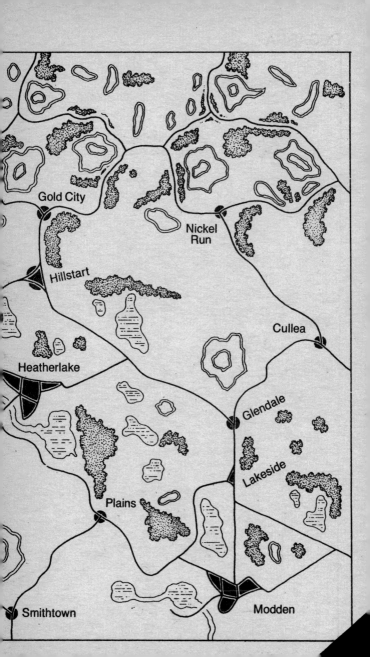

INTRODUCTION
by Bill Fawcett

You are in command. With the recorded blare of trumpets accented by a non-com's hurriedly barked order, it's back to battle for the Slammers. Mounting their tanks and skimmers are your men, highly trained mercenaries, whose lives depend upon the decisions you are about to make.

Slammers Down! provides more than just another chance to read an exciting military adventure featuring Hammer's Slammers. You could simply "read" this book, tracing a route through the sections, but these books are also a "game" which lets you make the command decisions.

This book is divided into sections rather than chapters. In each section of this game/book a military situation is described. Your choices actually write the book, both the story and the ending being determined by the combat decisions you make.

A careful effort has been made to make these adventures as "real" as possible. You are given the same information as you would receive in a real combat situation. At the end of each section is a number of choices for what to order next. The consequences of the action you pick are described in the following section. When you make the right decisions, you are closer to completing your mission successfully. When you make a bad decision, tanks burn and men die . . . men who are not going to be available for the next battle.

FIGHTING BATTLES

This book includes a simple game system, which simulates combat and other military challenges. Playing the game adds an extra dimension of enjoyment by making you a participant in the adventure. You will need two six-sided dice, a pencil and a sheet of paper to "play" along with this adventure.

COMBAT VALUES

In this book the force you command will consist of one force of tanks and one force of infantry skimmers. Each force is assigned five values. These values provide the means of comparing the capabilities of the many different military units encountered in this book. These five values are:

Manpower

This value is the number of separate fighting parts of your force. Each unit of Manpower represents one man, one tank, or whatever is firing. Casualties are subtracted from Manpower.

Ordnance

The quality and power of the weapons used is reflected by their Ordnance Value. All members of a unit commanded will have the same Ordnance Value. In some cases you may command two or more units, each with a different Ordnance Value.

Attack Strength

This value indicates the ability of the unit to attack an opponent. It is determined by multiplying Manpower by Ordnance (Manpower × Ordnance = Attack Strength). This value can be different for every battle. It will decrease as Manpower is lost and increase if reinforcements are received.

Melee Strength

This is the hand-to-hand combat value of each member of the unit. In the case of a squad of mercenaries, it represents the martial-arts skill and training of each man. In crewed units such as tanks or spaceships, it represents the fighting ability of the members of the crew and could be used in an assault on a spaceport or to defend against boarders. Melee Value replaces Ordnance Value when determining the Attack Strength of a unit in hand-to-hand combat.

Stealth

This value measures how well the members of your unit can avoid detection. It represents the individual skill of each soldier or the Electronic Counter Measures (ECM) of each spaceship. The Stealth Value for your unit will be the same for each member of the unit. You would employ stealth to avoid detection by the enemy.

Morale

This value reflects the fighting spirit of the troops you command. Success in battle may raise this value. Unpopular decisions or severe losses can lower it. If you order your unit to attempt something unusually dangerous, the outcome may be affected by their morale level.

THE COMBAT PROCEDURE

When your unit finds itself in a combat situation, use the following procedure to determine victory or defeat.

1. Compute the Attack Strength of your unit and the opposition. (Manpower × Ordnance or Melee Value = Attack Strength).
2. Turn to the charts at the end of this section which are given in the description of the battle.
3. Roll two six-sided dice and total the result.
4. Find the Attack Strength of the unit at the top of the chart and the total of the dice rolled on the left-hand column of the chart. The number found where the column and row intersect is the number of casualties inflicted by the unit you were rolling for onto their opponent.
5. Repeat for each side, alternating attacks.

The unit you command always fires first unless otherwise stated.

When you are told there is a combat situation, you will be given all the information needed for both your command and the opponent.

If two types of vehicles (tanks and skimmers) are fighting as one force, compute the attack value for each and total the results. Losses should alternate between each type, with the skimmer mounted infantry taking the first loss.

Here is an example of a complete combat:

Hammer's Slammers have come under fire from a force defending a ridge which crosses their line of advance. Alois Hammer has ordered your company of tanks to attack. Your tanks have an Ordnance Value of 8 and you have a Manpower Value of 8 tanks.

Slammers fire using Chart B.

Locals fire using chart D with a Combat Strength of 3 and Manpower of 12 (This gives them an Attack Strength of "36").

To begin, you attack first and roll two *4s* for a total of 8. The current Attack Strength of your Slammers is 64 (8 × 8).

CHART B

Attack Strength

					Manpower					
Dice Roll	1–10	–20	–30	–40	–50	–60	–70	–80	–90	–100	101+
2	0	0	0	1	1	1	2	2	2	3	4
3	0	0	1	1	1	2	2	2	3	3	4
4	0	1	1	1	2	2	2	3	3	3	4
5	1	1	1	2	2	2	3	3	3	4	5
6	1	1	2	2	2	3	3	3	4	4	5
7	1	2	2	2	3	3	3	4	4	4	5
8	2	2	2	3	3	3	4	4	4	5	6
9	2	2	3	3	3	4	4	4	5	5	6
10	2	3	3	3	4	4	4	5	5	5	6
11	3	3	3	4	4	4	5	5	5	6	7
12	3	3	4	4	4	5	5	6	6	7	8

Read down to 70 Attack Strength column until you get to the line for a dice roll of 8. The result is 4 casualties inflicted on your opponents by your company.

Subtract these casualties from the opposing force before determining their Attack Strength. (Combat is not simultaneous.) After subtracting the 4 casualties your company just inflicted on them, the enemy has a remaining Manpower Value of 8 (12 − 4 = 8). This gives them a remaining Attack Value of 24 (8 × 3 = 24).

Roll two six-sided dice for the opposing force's attack and determine the casualties they cause your Slammers company. Subtract these casualties from you Manpower total on the Record Sheet. In this case they caused one casualty, giving the Slammers a Manpower of 7 for the next round of combat.

This ends one "round" of combat. Repeat the process for each round. Each time a unit receives a casualty, it will have a lower value for Attack Strength. There will be that many fewer men, tanks, spaceships, or whatever firing.

Continue alternating fire rolls, recalculating the Attack Strength each time to account for casualties, until one side or the other has lost all of its Manpower, or special conditions (given in the text) apply. When this occurs, the battle is over.

Losses are permanent and losses from your unit should be subtracted from their total Manpower on the record sheet.

SNEAKING, HIDING AND OTHER RECKLESS ACTS

To determine if a unit is successful in any attempt relating to stealth or morale, roll two six-sided dice. If the total rolled is greater than the value listed for the unit, the attempt fails. If the total of the two dice is the same as or less than the current value, the attempt succeeds or the action goes undetected. For example:

Rico decides his squad of Mobile Infantry (MI) will try to penetrate the Bug hole unseen. MI have a stealth value of 8. A roll of 8 or less on two six-sided dice is needed to succeed. The dice are rolled and the result is a 4 and a 2 for a total of 6. They are able to avoid detection by the Bug guards.

If all of this is clear, then you are ready to turn to Section 1, meet with Alois Hammer, and take command.

COMBAT GROUP FOXTROT
(see also Appendix A)

Hovertanks (8 to begin)
☐ ☐ ☐ ☐ ☐ ☐ ☐ ☐
Ordnance: 4
Stealth: 4

Skimmer Infantry Squads
(12 to begin)
☐ ☐ ☐ ☐ ☐ ☐
☐ ☐ ☐ ☐ ☐ ☐
Ordnance: 2
Stealth: 8
Morale: 9
Notes:

Unless otherwise specified, both units will attack. Total both of their attack values together before rolling. When both types of units are involved alternate casualties, infantry is first.

THE COMBAT CHARTS

After you have made a decision involving a battle, you will be told which chart should be used for your unit and which for the enemy. The chart used is determined by the tactical and strategic situation. Chart A is used when the unit is most effective and Chart G when least effective. Chart A represents the effectiveness of the Sioux at Little Bighorn and Chart F, Custer. Chart G represents the equivalent of classic Zulus with aseiges (spears) versus modern Leopard tanks. Even a very small force on Chart A can be effective, while even a large number of combatants attacking on Chart G are unlikely to have much effect.

CHART A

Dice Roll	Attack Strength										
	1–10	–20	–30	–40	–50	–60	–70	–80	–90	–100	101 +
2	0	1	1	2	2	3	3	4	5	6	6
3	0	1	2	2	2	3	4	5	6	7	7
4	1	2	2	2	3	3	4	5	6	7	8
5	2	2	2	3	3	4	5	5	6	7	8
6	2	2	2	3	4	4	5	6	7	7	8
7	2	2	3	4	4	5	5	6	7	8	8
8	2	3	3	4	4	5	6	6	7	8	9
9	3	3	4	4	5	5	6	7	8	8	9
10	3	4	4	5	5	6	7	7	8	9	10
11	3	4	4	5	6	6	7	8	9	10	11
12	4	4	5	6	7	7	8	9	10	11	12

CHART B

Dice Roll	1–10	–20	–30	–40	–50	–60	–70	–80	–90	–100	101 +
2	0	0	0	1	1	1	2	2	2	3	4
3	0	0	1	1	1	2	2	2	3	3	4
4	0	1	1	1	2	2	2	3	3	3	4
5	1	1	1	2	2	2	3	3	3	4	5
6	1	1	2	2	2	3	3	3	4	4	5
7	1	2	2	2	3	3	3	4	4	4	5
8	2	2	2	3	3	3	4	4	4	5	6
9	2	2	3	3	3	4	4	4	5	5	6
10	2	3	3	3	4	4	4	5	5	5	6
11	3	3	3	4	4	4	5	5	5	6	7
12	3	3	4	4	4	5	5	6	6	7	8

CHART C

Dice Roll	1–10	–20	–30	–40	–50	–60	–70	–80	–90	–100	101+
2	0	0	0	0	0	1	1	1	2	2	2
3	0	0	0	0	1	1	1	2	2	2	3
4	0	0	0	1	1	1	2	2	2	3	3
5	0	0	1	1	1	2	2	2	3	3	4
6	0	1	1	1	2	2	2	3	3	3	4
7	1	1	1	2	2	2	3	3	3	4	5
8	1	1	2	2	2	3	3	3	4	4	5
9	1	2	2	2	3	3	3	4	4	5	5
10	2	2	2	3	3	3	4	4	4	5	6
11	2	2	3	3	3	4	4	4	5	5	6
12	2	3	3	3	4	4	4	5	5	6	7

CHART D

Dice Roll	1–10	–20	–30	–40	–50	–60	–70	–80	–90	–100	101+
2	0	0	0	0	0	0	0	1	1	1	2
3	0	0	0	0	0	0	1	1	1	2	2
4	0	0	0	0	0	1	1	1	2	2	2
5	0	0	0	0	1	1	1	2	2	2	3
6	0	0	0	1	1	1	2	2	2	3	3
7	0	0	1	1	1	2	2	2	3	3	4
8	0	1	1	1	2	2	2	3	3	4	4
9	1	1	1	2	2	2	3	3	3	4	5
10	1	1	2	2	2	3	3	3	4	4	5
11	1	2	2	2	3	3	3	4	4	5	5
12	2	2	2	3	3	3	4	4	5	5	6

CHART E

Dice Roll	1–10	–20	–30	–40	–50	–60	–70	–80	–90	–100	101+
2	0	0	0	0	0	0	0	0	0	1	1
3	0	0	0	0	0	0	0	0	1	1	1
4	0	0	0	0	0	0	0	1	1	1	2
5	0	0	0	0	0	0	1	1	1	2	2
6	0	0	0	0	0	1	1	1	1	2	2
7	0	0	0	0	1	1	1	1	2	2	2
8	0	0	0	1	1	1	1	2	2	2	2
9	0	0	1	1	1	1	2	2	2	2	2
10	0	1	1	1	1	2	2	2	2	2	3
11	1	1	1	1	2	2	2	2	2	2	3
12	1	1	1	2	2	2	2	2	2	3	3

CHART F

Dice Roll	1–10	–20	–30	–40	–50	–60	–70	–80	–90	–100	101+
2	0	0	0	0	0	0	0	0	0	0	0
3	0	0	0	0	0	0	0	0	0	0	0
4	0	0	0	0	0	0	0	0	0	0	0
5	0	0	0	0	0	0	0	0	0	0	0
6	0	0	0	0	0	0	0	0	0	0	1
7	0	0	0	0	0	0	0	0	0	0	1
8	0	0	0	0	0	0	0	0	0	1	1
9	0	0	0	0	0	0	0	0	1	1	1
10	0	0	0	0	0	0	0	1	1	1	1
11	1	1	1	1	1	1	1	1	1	1	2
12	1	1	1	1	1	1	1	1	1	2	3

CHART G

	1–10	–20	–30	–40	–50	–60	–70	–80	–90	–100	101+
Dice Roll											
2	0	0	0	0	0	0	0	0	0	0	0
3	0	0	0	0	0	0	0	0	0	0	0
4	0	0	0	0	0	0	0	0	0	0	0
5	0	0	0	0	0	0	0	0	0	0	0
6	0	0	0	0	0	0	0	0	0	0	0
7	0	0	0	0	0	0	0	0	0	0	0
8	0	0	0	0	0	0	0	0	0	0	0
9	0	0	0	0	0	0	0	0	0	0	0
10	0	0	0	0	0	0	0	0	0	0	1
11	0	0	0	0	0	0	0	0	0	1	1
12	1	1	1	1	1	1	1	1	1	1	1

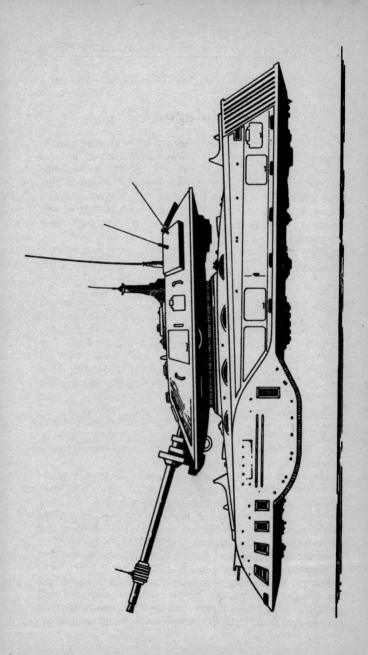

— Prologue —

First envisioned as slow-moving fortresses to creep through the muck of the First World War, tanks matured into the daringly fast panzers of the Second World War, but with the invention of the anti-tank missile, appeared poised to sink into oblivion by the end of the twentieth century. As man leaped to the stars, fools hoped that he would leave war behind him. But wherever there is need, there is want. So it was among the stars.

Those same tools that had helped man to conquer the stars helped man to once again eclipse the Queen of Battle. With the advent of portable fusion reactors, tanks were no longer limited by tracks—an earlier liability. Now they had the energy to lift themselves on air and hover above the ground, traversing areas previously impenetrable. Powerguns gave the new supertanks more punch than imaginable, while complex computer links gave the guns more range and flexibility than ever even dreamed. Still, the need was small and the want not frequent enough for most planets to consider building these masters of battle. So the need was filled by mercenaries. The best mercenaries could afford the best tanks.

And the best mercenaries were in the regiment of Colonel Alois Hammer. The best were also the most expensive. Many planets hired inferior mercenaries or did without. Those that could hire "Hammer's Slammers" were assured of victory—provided they could pay for it.

The expense of mercenaries was such that planets sometimes contemplated reneging on their contracts. There was also the chance that the mercenaries might consider filling in their own names on the line marked "victor." To prevent either misfortune, the Bonding Authority came into being as a powerful force for fair dealing. The authority had been known to reduce to rubble planets that broke their contracts, and also to eliminate mercenary regiments failing to honor theirs. Still, with every bureaucracy there is a certain inertia to action, and the thought of a mistake by the Bonding Authority was enough to give planet leaders, mercenary commanders, and the members of the Authority themselves recurrent nightmares.

— 1 —

Bull Bromley paced the room, counting the four paces to himself unconsciously. As he reached one end, he made a smart rear march and continued on without pausing. His rugged features were slack, his eyes vacant and body forgotten as he asked himself again and again why he had done it.

There were two cots in the room. Shelves with some cans still on them betrayed the fact that this was once a storage room. The cots had been thrown in as hastily as the two men, and were neat with clean sheets and blankets; the men were disheveled, with cuts and torn uniforms. The second man appeared perhaps more disheveled than Bull Bromley, but little could be discerned at the moment since he was face-down, asleep on his cot.

First Lieutenant Braddington "Bull" Bromley knew what the face of the other man would look like. He had no doubt that the man had a whopping black eye, because he had put it there. He also knew that his parade-dress uniform was ruined beyond repair, and that never in the history of the regiment had any such thing occurred.

Pacing, he thought back to the start of his troubles, when Hammer's Slammers first came to this planet and its war.

Maffren was a jewel among the heavens. With its large metal deposits and lush lands, it was no wonder that many were attracted to the planet. All who came later placed second to the original colony ship. The newcomers found themselves in need of food and shelter that only the original colonists could provide. And, like every new planet, Maffren had dangers that only experience could expose.

It was perhaps to be expected that settlers arriving on Maffren after the original colonists found themselves in both financial and spiritual debt to those who had come first. Over the years the hold of the First Ones over the Laters became more pronounced and less benevolent. When iridium was discovered in the craggy peaks of Parradayne, none of the rich First Ones were inclined to investigate, preferring the comfort of their ancestor's wealth. Newer blood, some coming fresh on planet, explored the Crags of Parradayne and shed blood for every mistake.

These Crageens, as settled folk in Maffren called them, did not see why they should pay any of the "thanks" that the First Ones levied on the planet. Disagreement escalated until force was used. In their mountainous country, the Crageens were difficult foes, but they had no skill in pitched battle.

The situation stagnated for several decades until many of the lowland Laters also began to question their need to pay "thanks." A full-scale war bloomed as many of the Laters joined the Crageens in rebelling against the rule of the First Ones.

The fighting blood of the First Ones had thinned while their wealth had grown. They sent for Colonel Hammer's regiment. The price was right.

News of their decision quickly reached the men of the Crag Mountains. Their wealth was scarcer although potentially the greater. But no mercenary unit would consider such potential payment. No unit except one.

Jebbitt's Raiders had once been an acceptable outfit. They still were, according to the Bonding Authority. The fact that they left their last job with more haste than was thought necessary, and that there was still an investigation into the handling of their last contract (nuclear weapons had become exceedingly unpopular) was of little import. But even though they had nuked with little concern over whom they hit, the Raiders had not been on the side of the victors in their last battle. They were, in a word, desperate. Desperate enough to take on the Slammers on the promise of a percentage of the spoils.

They lost . . . badly. *Badly* can have several meanings, and the Raiders explored most of them. They lost almost all of their equipment. They lost many men, and they lost their respect for the most fragile of conventions: the Rules of War.

There is a town on the plains of Tegara where no one will smile again. Their jaws were all shot off.

There is a town in the high crags of Kiltoween where no children will ever be born again. All the males were castrated and all the women impaled.

In spite of such atrocities and their desperate attempts to wrest money from the poor and war-trodden, the Raiders lost. They lost so badly that, even on the eve of their last battle, when Gesparde Jebbitt, self-styled General of Maffren, proclaimed that he would inflict the same calamity on the Slammers that had been "inflicted on my gallant men," those self-same gallant men vanished.

Or rather, they attempted to vanish. Slammer's Team Foxtrot barred the way. Of the five thousand men who formed Jebbitt's Raiders, four thousand found themselves surrounded by a bristling hive of tanks and skimmers that had inexplicably appeared in their line of retreat. The "Fighting Fox" had done it again. Two platoons, just four tanks and four squads of infantry, had outwitted the might of Jebbitt's Raiders.

The members of Team Foxtrot were not supermen. They merely applied once again the lessons of Guderian and O'Connor by being where their enemy knew they could not be. They had gone by back roads and taken many detours. They had foregone sleep and food to get where they had to be, where First Lieutenant Bull Bromley said they had to be.

So the war ended. Colonel Hammer decided to retain the two platoons of Team Foxtrot with the Training Battalion for a week while the remainder of the Slammers embarked for their new contract on Darien. Training time was hard to come by, and Hammer would also be able to see how suited Bromley was to a company of his own. If Colonel Hammer had other reasons, he didn't mention them.

Other problems concerned him in the interim. The damned freighters were late again, and his forward intelligence units were once again giving him the gloomy truth about the new contract they would soon work. While the bulk of the Slammers awaited their transport, Hammer decreed that Team Foxtrot and other select units could take a four-day pass.

With stern warnings and some jokes, Bull Bromley had released his proud men for their pass. The people of Maffren were willing hosts. Second Lieutenant Peter Smyth had joined him shortly afterwards, having similarly released his infantry platoon. They knew where they were going, both of them to the same place: a small town at the base of the hills called Cullea. But they had both gone to see the same woman.

Smyth had seen Bull walking up the path to Donna Mills's house. If Bull had seen Smyth first, the fight might never have happened. Bromley had won the fight—at least he was still standing and Pete Smyth wasn't. He had been about to do what he'd set out to do when a detachment from Security, doubtless called by worried townspeople, arrived on the scene.

And now he was here, pacing the small space. It had been a supply room before being hastily converted into a cell. Pete Smyth still lay facedown on his bunk. Bromley wondered if he could ever work with Smyth again, or worse, if either of them would ever *work* again, especially after Smyth had slept through the huge explosion that awoke Bull.

Bromley wondered what had caused the explosion. It didn't sound like one on the transports lifting. He'd slept through enough of them already that night. Yet it didn't sound like artillery or small-arms fire. The sound of keys jangling in the lock broke his musing. The door opened to reveal Security Sergeant Mungren. He was looking strangely perturbed.

"The Colonel wants to see you two immediately," Mungren explained. With a glance to the other cot he added, "Better wake up the lieutenant, sir."

Bromley nodded and nudged Smyth. Startled, Smyth's hands came up to combat ready as Bromley explained, "The Colonel wants us."

Smyth's eyebrows raised in surprise. "Already? I thought he would let us stew awhile."

Outside, Bromley was struck by the unusual amount of activity in the camp. A glance from Smyth confirmed his opinion that the normal activity of embarkation had been augmented by something else, something that added a frantic note. The amount of activity around the communications shack was awesome.

The two guards outside Colonel Hammer's office came to attention as the officers passed by, causing Bromley to wonder if they'd behave the same way when he returned. Colonel Hammer gave the two men only a cursory glance when they entered, motioning to the aide who was talking with him to leave. Bromley pulled himself to attention and rendered a clean salute. He sensed Pete Smyth doing the same a few feet to his rear, but Colonel Hammer did not return their salute. After a few moments he snorted and tossed off the most indifferent salute anyone had ever seen him give.

"At ease," he growled. Bromley and Smyth relaxed a trifle, only to tense again as Hammer continued. "You two ought to be proud of yourselves!" With a bang of his fist, he added, "Stars' sake! I was going to promote you!

"It doesn't matter now," he continued. "I've got a mission for you. If half the regiment weren't already en route to Darien, I'd keep you locked up until you were screaming, but they are and I'm in a hurry. Besides,'' he added in a different tone, ''you two were the best team we ever had.''

An expression of intense pain and sorrow crossed his face. ''One of the . . .'' He paused. ''One of our transports has crashed. The *Vindictive* was carrying two tank companies, a company of combat cars, and an infantry company. We've had word from the survivors. The situation is grim.''

''Sir!'' The words were torn from Bromley's mouth. His friends were on those transports, maybe even his troops.

''Not yours, Bromley,'' the Colonel reassured him. ''Part of your company all the same. But that platoon sergeant of yours, Lewis, wouldn't let me load your platoon until either charges were brought or you were released. I nearly had him put in with you!''

''The wreck of the transport is bad enough,'' he continued. ''I've got wounded men out there, lieutenants, men who *don't* fight with each other.'' Again a painful pause. ''We've also heard reports that some of our former enemy have decided that the war isn't over yet. They're attacking the survivors.''

''From what we can gather, the wreckage is strewn over a wide area. Most of our tanks are buried in the wreckage. The few that are in operation are without ammo. Our men are running out of small arms ammunition and are desperately in need of medical supplies.''

Colonel Hammer is leading up to something.

If Bull lets him continue, turn to section 2.

If Bull volunteers to lead a rescue mission, turn to section 3.

— 2 —

Colonel Hammer paused. After a long moment he said, "I hoped that you would be able to figure out what I was trying to say, Lieutenant Bromley. I want you and Lieutenant Smyth to volunteer to lead the rescue mission."

If Bull volunteers for the mission, turn to section 5.

If Bull declines the mission, turn to section 4.

— 3 —

The Old Man didn't have to spell it out. Bull hadn't gotten his nickname for being stupid.

"Sir," he replied. "If my men are here and ready, I know that they'll want to help. Let us rescue the Slammers."

Turn to section 6.

— 4 —

"Sir, you have placed me under arrest for striking a fellow officer. I am under no obligation by military law to perform any duties," Bull told Hammer sternly.

An exclamation of incredulity and disgust burst forth from Pete Smyth. With a glance of pure disdain for Bromley, the young infantry lieutenant cried, "I'll go, sir!"

Hammer appeared surprised. "Lieutenant Bromley, I thought better of you. It is apparent to me now that the true spirit of Team Foxtrot is that of your subordinates.

"I shall not force you to go. Rather, I shall make your

decision part of the testimony in your upcoming court martial and recommend the maximum penalty for your crime. And if . . . if by some strange chance you are found not guilty, I shall immediately discharge you from the Slammers." Then in a cold voice he added, "We do not tolerate cowards." Angrily, he turned to Sergeant Mungren. "Take this man back to the guardhouse and leave him there!"

Because Lieutenant Bromley stood firm on his rights, many of his comrades will die. He has disgraced himself, his unit, and the regiment of Colonel Alois Hammer. He is probably worse than dead.

Stop!

If you choose to play again, return to section 1 and make different choices.

— 5 —

Bull Bromley might not be quick on his feet, but he is loyal. "Of course we'll volunteer, sir. It's what a Slammer has to do."

"Good," the Colonel agreed. "I was hoping to hear you say that. You two are the only officers I have right now capable of leading such a mission." He turned to Smyth. "You may as well give the warning order to the men, Lieutenant. While you're at it, stop by Operations and see if they have any news for us."

Second Lieutenant Pete Smyth gave Colonel Hammer a sharp salute that seemed out of place with his tattered uniform. With a brisk stride he left the Colonel's office.

As Bromley started to follow him, Colonel Hammer raised a hand. "One moment, Lieutenant. I heard about the reason for the fight you two had. I don't approve." He paused. "Lieutenant Smyth is young and probably won't stay in service with us, but I took you for a career man. I guess I was wrong." After a moment he added, "I might be wrong in sending you two out now after what happened. If you don't trust Smyth or you can't work with him, say the word now

and I'll have him relieved. Young Beirne's his platoon sergeant. He'll do the job almost as well." He looked Bromley
in the eye. "Just say the word and I'll have Smyth sent back
to the guardhouse."

Hammer's eyes pinned him, demanding an instant answer.
Time was critical. Bull found himself contemplating two
images: the haggard, grinning face of Pete Smyth as they
finished their last battle with the Raiders; and the scowling,
angry face of Pete Smyth as he tried to beat Bull into the
ground.

If Bull removes Pete Smyth from command, turn to section 7.

*If Bull decides to keep Pete in command of the infantry
platoon of Team Foxtrot, turn to section 8.*

— 6 —

"Excellent, Lieutenant! I hoped to hear you say that!"
Colonel Hammer replied. "I'm going to need someone out
there with his wits about him." He turned to Smyth. "And
what about you, Lieutenant Smyth?"

"Of course, sir. You shouldn't have to ask," Smyth replied. Bromley raised an eyebrow at his second-in-command,
wondering if perhaps Smyth wasn't being a bit too testy.

The Colonel paused for a moment, as if to consider Smyth's
reply. "Very well, lieutenant," he agreed. "Why don't you
issue the warning order to the men and check in at Operations
while you're at it?"

Smyth saluted and briskly left the tent.

"I heard about the reason for your fracas," Hammer said.
"I don't like it. But now I'm wondering . . ." He shrugged.
"I don't have time. If you don't trust Smyth, tell me and I'll
replace him. Simon Beirne's his platoon sergeant and an able
man."

Bull Bromley recalled the times he and Pete Smyth had
worked together, the extreme conciseness of their actions, the
way in which they had almost seemed to think the same
thoughts. It was this unique blend of tank speed and infantry

doggedness that had made Team Foxtrot a legend even in the Slammers. Bromley had thought that it would never end—until last night.

If Bull removes Pete Smyth from command, turn to section 7.

If Bull decides to keep Smyth in command of the infantry platoon of Team Foxtrot, turn to section 8.

— **7** —

Last night had ended it all. No matter what the provocation, Pete Smyth had hit him. Bromley shook his head slowly.

"No sir. I can't work with him anymore," he said, raising his head to meet Hammer eye to eye. "I don't care about the right or wrong of it. I just don't think that he'll do what I want when I need it."

Colonel Hammer sighed. "I wasn't sure. I don't know what I'd do in your situation." He locked eyes with the sturdy lieutenant. For an instant Bromley was reminded of a great cat pondering whether to pounce. Then Hammer's eyes softened.

"Very well. Smyth will be replaced." Then in a harder tone of voice he added, "Heaven help you if you fail, because I'll be the first to post bounty on your hide!"

"I won't fail, sir," Bromley replied.

"Damn straight you won't," Hammer agreed. "Now get out of here. Tell my orderly to come in on your way out. He has to talk to a young lieutenant."

But before Bromley could turn to leave, Pete Smyth came rushing back in with news from Operations. He started to speak but caught the look in Bromley's eyes. As if for confirmation, he turned to the Colonel.

The Colonel glanced at Bromley silently asking: Are you really sure? Then the Colonel told Smyth, "There's been a change of plans. You aren't going on the mission. Tell your platoon sergeant that he's to take charge of your platoon."

Stunned, Smyth froze stock-still, shoulders slumped in despair. Then he recovered, snapped to attention and said, "I'm sure Sergeant Beirne will do an excellent job, sir. I've trained him for it." After a moment he added, "With your permission?"

Smyth executed a perfect salute at the Colonel's nod, performed an about-face, and marched out of the office. The effect was marred only by the look of pure hatred that he directed toward Lieutenant Bromley as he caught his eye.

There was a moment of silence as the two men recovered from their interruption. It was broken by a tense, soft growl from Hammer. "You'd better not fail, Bromley!"

For a moment Bull wondered if he should recall his decision, but it was too late. The die was cast.

"I'll get the word from Operations on my way out, sir," Bromley stated. At the Colonel's nod, Bull left.

The orderly murmur of Operations dropped a level as Bromley entered. Many knew that he had been chosen for the mission, and some also knew that he had turned down Smyth as second-in-command. Before anyone could engage him in conversation, Major Pritchard separated from the crowd and approached him.

"We haven't got much time, Bromley," Pritchard said immediately. "I've organized a convoy of softskinned vehicles under Sergeant Major Ogren. They'll follow immediately behind your combat group. For that reason, you've got to stick pretty much to the roads." He grimaced. "Sorry I couldn't get armored transports to follow up, but we've already shipped almost everything."

"Artillery?" Bromley asked.

Pritchard shook his head. "Gone. And the satellite network is already in place on Darien. This was unexpected."

"So what do I have?" Bromley asked.

"You've got your tank platoon, Lieutenant Smyth's infantry platoon led by Sergeant Beirne, as well as two training infantry platoons and one training tank platoon." Pritchard ticked each off on his fingers. "I've tried to get at least one combat-experienced person on each vehicle, but we're spread too thin. I can't even get enough medical personnel." An aide gestured at him hurriedly. "Excuse me, that'll be the mayor on the comm. I asked for medical help from the townspeople."

Write the word "Smyth" on a piece of paper to note that you have had Lieutenant Smyth removed from command.

Time is critical, and Major Pritchard is urgently needed elsewhere to coordinate the rescue mission.

If Bull leaves now, turn to section 9.

If Bull questions Major Pritchard further, turn to section 10.

— 8 —

Bromley shook his head clear of such thoughts. "That won't be necessary, sir. I've never known Lieutenant Smyth to put personal situations above his men or the other Slammers."

"But will he obey you?" Hammer asked coldly.

"I'm willing to bet on it," Bull told him.

Hammer stroked his chin in thought. He started to say something more but Bromley stopped him.

"Sir, Foxtrot's been a team. It's been a team because I can depend on Pete Smyth to obey my orders even if he knows some of his men are going to get killed because of them." Bromley swallowed. "Even after last night, he still knows that I'll never needlessly sacrifice him or his men. He'll obey me, sir."

"Very well, Lieutenant," Hammer agreed. "I hope your faith is well founded." He paused. "*My* men will die if you're wrong."

Before Hammer could say anything more, Smyth rushed in with news from Operations. His purposeful stride had a tense air to it. With one look, Bromley gathered that Smyth had guessed their conversation. A tentative smile played across Smyth's lips.

"What are you so happy about, Lieutenant?" Hammer snarled.

"Sergeant Major Ogren is leading the softskinned vehicles in the rescue convoy, sir!" Smyth retorted instantly.

"Is he?" Hammer growled, then softer: "He is? Good. That means that at least you won't have to worry about your ass."

Sergeant Major Ogren was a legend in the Slammers. He had turned down a commission so many times that it was rumored Colonel Hammer had threatened to retire him if he did it again. Rumor also had it that Ogren's reply was immediate: "And who'll run your regiment then?" Ogren was known to lecture young lieutenants with his fists. It was whispered that Ogren had trained Hammer himself.

"What are the rest of our forces?" Bromley inquired.

"Your platoon of tanks, another from Training, my infantry platoon and two more from Training," Smyth ticked off on his fingers. The look he gave Bromley was grim. "I couldn't get much more from Major Pritchard, sir. He was busy trying to arrange medical support from the civilians—we don't have enough."

"Eight tanks, twelve squads of skimmers! Damn!" Hammer swore. "I'll never be caught with my pants down like this again!"

Pete Smyth gave the Colonel a worried look.

"It's not that bad," Bromley corrected. "You've got my Team Foxtrot plus Foxtrot Alpha Tango, Foxtrot Alpha India, and Foxtrot Bravo India. Those are the three fully equipped training platoons, right, Smyth?"

"Yes sir!"

"I fail to see the reason for your confidence," Hammer replied flatly. "The training troops haven't seen combat, most of their officers and non-coms have just been promoted, and you haven't been on exercises with them yet."

"Yes sir!" Smyth agreed. "But the two infantry officers were sergeants in my forward squads. You gave them battlefield promotions. And the lieutenant in charge of Foxtrot Alpha Tango platoon was the track commander who held the pass against Jebbitt's retreat."

"That is better," Hammer agreed. "But they're still green."

"I agree, sir," Bromley replied. "This isn't the best time to put people into a new position. They need all the time they can get. If you'll excuse me, I'm going to do my best to provide it."

Hammer returned their salutes, and they departed.

Time is of the essense.

If Bull decides to go immediately to his assembled forces, turn to section 9.

If Bull decides to consult with Operations first, turn to section 10.

— 9 —

As he crossed the compound, Bull was engulfed in the whine of hover fans straining to hold their tanks' bulk centimeters above the ground. Ahead of him was arrayed a force that always made Bull's heart beat faster: Lariat Two, second platoon of L Company, four of the best-crewed, fastest-moving, best-hitting tanks in Hammer's regiment. M Company might lead, but L Company was always called on to clean up. And Bull's second platoon was always the first to clean up. Braddington Bromley was halfway to the massing tanks when a skimmer pulled up beside him.

"Need a ride?" The familiar, soft, half-hoarse voice of Platoon Sergeant Sam "Lightnin' " Lewis reassured Bull immediately. Sergeant Lewis had come from Earth itself and had taken a drop in rank to get into the Slammers. Bull had never seen Lewis lose his temper.

"When are you going to get a job?" Bull responded.

"When you make captain," Lewis replied. Then, all business, he said, "This doesn't look like an easy one."

"Tell me about it," Bull agreed.

"Sure, climb aboard. Your corporal's all worried about you," Lewis told him as he mounted the little skimmer.

"Okay, Sam, give me your rundown." Braddington Bromley had been a corporal when Lewis was a green private. He knew when Lewis was apprehensive.

"You haven't been listening to the net, have you, sir?" Lewis asked. Not needing Bull's answer, he continued, "Well, there's a lot of confusion out there. There are a lot of our men in pain, too. What's worrying me are the reports that civilians are firing on them, old rebels starting back up again. Other reports say that it's the Raiders."

Bull cocked an eyebrow. "And you think . . . ?"

Lewis shook his head. "I don't know, sir. I just don't know." The skimmer slowed to a stop. "Here we are."

If Bull removed Lieutenant Smyth from command, turn to section 11.

If Bull kept Lieutenant Smyth in command of the infantry platoon, turn to section 12.

— 10 —

The noise of the Operations room stilled as Bromley asked Major Pritchard, "What's your assessment of the situation, Major?"

Pritchard gave Bromley a searching glance. "I don't like it, Bull," he said. "There are something odd about the way the transport went down. There are indications of an explosion.

"Further, the transport debris is spread over a wide area. I don't have contact with every unit that I knew was aboard. I'm getting sparse and contradictory communications from the crash site. Either there are a lot of confused people out there or . . . I don't know. We don't have any satellite cover, no artillery. You're on your own." Pritchard sketched the military scene swiftly.

"Fortunately," he continued, "your computer maps are still set up for this terrain, unlike the rest of our equipment on the transport. There are three main routes: north to the beginning of the Crageens, then west; northwest straight through the plains; and west then north, skirting the forests all the way. There are connecting roads to each route. You've got about three hundred kilometers to cover. If you're quick and you don't have too much trouble, you'll be able to get there in under three hours." Pritchard shrugged. "That's all I know. Good luck!"

"Thank you, sir!" Bromley replied, and trotted briskly out of Operations.

Turn to section 9.

— 11 —

A group of men loitered around Bromley's tank, Lariat Two Six. Among them, Bromley recognized Colonel Hammer. He got off the skimmer and started toward the Colonel, but a figure in the crowd stepped in front of him and stopped him short. The figure was Smyth. When Hammer saw the confrontation, he closed the distance rapidly.

"Lieutenant Johnson is dead," Hammer said abruptly. He addressed Bull Bromley, but his words were for both lieutenants. "Johnson's skimmer ran into a civilian vehicle as he was rounding up the last of his men. Sergeant Santy is experienced, so I've given him charge of that platoon." Hammer sighed. "I can't let this mission go out with two platoons commanded by sergeants. Lieutenant Smyth is going. He's the only choice."

"I don't think I can trust him, sir," Bromley replied, fists clenched at his sides.

"You have no choice, Lieutenant!" Hammer snarled. "I won't have you jeopardize the lives of my men. If he disobeys you, shoot him!"

Without further word, Hammer stalked off.

Pete Smyth approached Bromley cautiously, and after a moment said, "I know your feelings in this situation, sir. I'll do my duty."

Bromley gave him a searching glance. "Do that. Men are depending on you." He looked around and called, "Sergeant Lewis!"

"Sir!" Sergeant Lewis hurried over.

"How soon can we move out?" Bull asked.

"Immediately," Lewis told him. "We need to know which route to take, of course, and the marching order." Smyth cleared his throat. Lewis glanced at him. "Sir?"

Looking at Lieutenant Bromley, Smyth said; "Under the circumstances, I wonder if emergency CEOIs aren't in order."

CEOIs, or Communications Equipment Operating Instructions, were used back in the days when military orders were transmitted by radio instead of laserlink, and subject to interception and deciphering. CEOIs were books that included code names for units and officers. These codes allowed orders to be given quickly and concisely, and prevented the enemy from interpreting them. Hammer's Slammers use laserlink communications systems which were completely secure, so CEOIs were almost never required. Even so, every tank and skimmer carried a book of them.

"There are many disadvantages to their use, sir," Lewis replied smoothly. "Most men don't know how to use them, so we'll lose valuable time. Your orders will have to be worded more carefully. I don't know if we can afford the confusion they'll create."

If Bull chooses to use emergency CEOIs, turn to section 13.

If Bull decides not to use emergency CEOIs, turn to section 14.

— 12 —

Bromley didn't dismount just then. "Your suggestions?" he asked.

Sergeant Lewis screwed up his face. "Get there quick. Choose a good route. If Jebbitt's Raiders got together again, you'd better choose a route they don't expect. Blitzkrieg 'em."

Pete Smyth approached just then. "Sergeant Lewis told me the whole story already, sir. I agree. I have one other suggestion, though." Bromley's cocked eyebrow encouraged him to continue. "I think we should take emergency CEOIs and use 'em."

"CEOIs?" Lewis inquired of the two officers.

"Communications Equipment Operating Instructions," Bromley explained. "Every tank and skimmer's got a book of them. In times when secure communications weren't possible, armed forces used codes. They included codes for each vehicle and unit. They take a bit of getting used to, but the enemy won't be able to decipher them easily."

"I don't like the idea, sir," Lewis replied. "If I don't

know about them, you can be sure none of the other non-coms are familiar with them, either. A new system could add trouble where we've got enough already.''

''That's true,'' Smyth agreed. ''But if the Raiders are out there, they could have some of our comm. equipment. They might even have caused that transport to crash. If that's the case, I don't think we should give them the chance to know what we're doing. We shouldn't even rely on the standard CEOIs. Let's set up emergency codes for this operation.''

If Bull chooses to set up special CEOIs, turn to section 13.

If Bull decides not to use special CEOIs, turn to section 14.

— 13 —

''We'll use special CEOIs,'' Bromley decided. ''Sergeant Lewis, see to it that all vehicles and squads have them. Make sure that the NCO's all read the instructions. We'll use them when I give the command signal 'Bluejay Five.' ''

''Bluejay Five?'' Lewis repeated. ''Very well, sir. I'll get right to that.''

Mark down ''Bluejay Five'' on your note paper to remind you that the CEOIs have been distributed.

Turn to section 15.

— 14 —

Bromley debated with himself. CEOIs would allow his combat group the ability to surprise the enemy, but the enemy knew where they were going so there was little advantage in surprise. Speed and concentrated power were what would could. He shook his head.

"No, I don't think it's worth it," he told the others. "But thanks, anyway, for the suggestion."

Turn to section 15.

— 15 —

"Follow me to my tank, Smyth," Bull said to his second-in-command. Bull clambered onto the huge tank with the grace of a mountain lion going up a cliff. His meaty hundred kilos did nothing to alter the rock-steady hovertank as it dusted the ground with its four huge fans. To Lewis he shouted, "Get all the platoon leaders here!"

"Right, sir!" Lewis shouted over his shoulder as he trotted to the rest of the vehicles.

Lewis was soon engulfed in a hive of activity as tankers and pongoes strove to get their gear on and their ammo loaded under the harsh encouragement of the granite-jawed Sergeant Major Ogren. Behind the hovertanks and skimmers, Bull saw masses of fragile wheeled vehicles—the softskinneds that would carry much needed supplies to the survivors.

Corporal Ennis, second in command of Bromley's tank, stuck his head out of a hatch on the turret of Lariat Two Six. He swiveled the navigational display up in the track commander's cupola so that Bromley could point out the terrain they had to traverse to the massing officers. For the first time Bromley got a decent picture of his choices. He could see immediately the three main routes to the wreck. There were also several chances to switch from one route to another along the way.

If Bull takes the central northwest road, turn to section 16.

If Bull starts out on the north road, turn to section 17.

If Bull chooses the route going west, then north, turn to section 18.

Lt. Bromley

— 16 —

The northwest road made the most sense, Bull finally decided. Going that way he had the chance to switch northward or westward if he ran into difficulties. The abundance of cities and fairly open spaces made it easy terrain to negotiate rapidly. Going that way would also avoid the potential pitfalls of the mountains on the northerly route and the forests of the westerly route.

His officers approached his tank expectantly. Bull glanced at Corporal Ennis, who gave him a knowing look and smiled.

"How much did you bet?" Bull asked his young corporal.

"I've got fifty credits riding on your taking the central route, sir," Corporal Ennis replied easily.

"I hope you made the overlays as well as you placed that bet," Bull told him.

"Yes indeed!" Ennis answered, displaying the carefully rolled clear overlays clenched in his right hand. "I'll bet you didn't think I'd've thought of it, sir."

"How much?" Bull asked.

"Hmm." Ennis frowned, stroking his chin. "Maybe you did think I'd do it."

"Maybe," Bull agreed. The lieutenants were now upon them. "Let's hope you did a good job."

"Yes sir." Ennis sobered. With a wave of his hand at the overlays he added, "These have got lives riding on them."

"Maybe ours," Bull agreed. Then he turned to face the officers below him. He scanned their faces, trying to divine their feelings. Dyer looked confident, almost cocky. Peyton was quiet and attentive. Bravo India's platoon leader was fidgety and obviously eager to impress and afraid to fail. To the massed officers he said, "Well, gentlemen, it appears that my corporal has taken on the abilities of a mind reader. I've promised him that I won't trade him to Intelligence just yet.

"We're going to be heading out of here by the central northwest route. I believe it'll be faster and allow us a greater chance to switch directions if we have to. Use the overlays

Corporal Ennis is handing out—hand them out now, Ennis—they'll provide us with a degree of security."

Bull managed to intercept a copy. "I see he's learned how to label phaselines. That might prove useful. One thing I must stress, gentlemen, is that we cannot afford to retreat out of any conflict. We have to clear the road for the softskinned vehicles Sergeant Major Ogren is leading. If they don't get through, this exercise is pointless."

He paused to let that message sink in. Then he looked at the overlays again. Slammers did not normally use phaselines, relying on instant computer displays to show the locations of all known enemy and friendly troops. Phaselines had been used extensively in the twentieth century by commanders not so equipped to keep track of the progress of their sub-elements. Without the satellites to spot for them, the Slammers were reduced to such primitive techniques. Each phaseline was drawn across a particular landmark, normally a town, and was used to let Bull know where his sub-elements were located.

"Our route takes us to a tee junction, left to the town of Plains and straight on to the city of Heatherlake. Those are phaselines Yellow, Aqua, and Green respectively. From there we'll either go west to Tooey, phaseline Amber, or continue north and finally west to the town of Regarra, phaseline Gold. The wreckage, phaseline Iridium, isn't too far away from that town. Are there any questions?"

"Yes sir," Lieutenant Peyton replied. "What's the order of march and what sort of formation are we using?"

Bull hadn't answered that question for himself yet. Obviously, now was the time to find the answer. While he could change the formation later, the need for speed would always conflict with the need for a good combat formation which conformed to the demands of the terrain. He outlined in his mind the formations he thought best suited: a tank shield with the skimmers close in behind his two platoons of panzers to keep them safe from small-arms fire, or a tank forward recon with the infantry poised to mop up any trouble.

If Lieutenant Bromley chooses to use the tank shield formation, turn to section 19.

If he chooses to send the tanks forward in recon, turn to section 20.

— 17 —

The lower route, skirting the forest, looked too deceptive to Bull. If there was going to be trouble, that route would be the way to find it. The central route was too predictable. Anyone would bet that he would come that way. Team Foxtrot, now Group Foxtrot, had never had a reputation for predictability. The upper route, going first north then west, presented the least obvious choice. It took them through mountainous terrain and the homes of the Crageens. They might not be so hostile now that the war was over and the Raiders had proved to be their worst enemy.

"Did you bet on this one, Ennis?" Bull asked his corporal.

"Me, sir? Bet?" Ennis tried his best to look innocent. "Heck sir, you're too hard to predict."

"But . . ." Bull supplied him.

"But if I was to bet, I'd've said that you'd take the plains route, sir. You know, go northwest straight to the wreck," Ennis finished.

Bull shook his head. "I'm glad you didn't bet. I hope you made overlays for the route through the mountains."

"The mountains!" Ennis swore. Bull nodded to himself. The corporal must have bet a packet. Ennis recovered from his shock and stammered, "Uh, yes sir. I have them here." Ennis groped inside the tank for them.

When the officers arrived, Bull told them, "We're going to the mountains." As they digested that information, he continued, "It's the last place we're expected to go. The Crageens aren't our friends, but their enemies are our enemies. I don't think they will have anything to do with Jebbitt's Raiders after the way they were treated.

"The corporal here is handing out—hand out those overlays, Ennis!—maps of our route." Bull snagged one of the overlays as Ennis extended it toward an officer. "I see my corporal has learned to put in phaselines. Good. We may use them."

He paused to let that message sink in. Then he looked at the overlays again. Slammers did not normally use phaselines, relying on instant computer displays to show the locations of all known enemy and friendly troops. Phaselines had been used extensively in the twentieth century by commanders not so equipped, to keep track of the progress of their sub-elements. Without the satellites to spot for them, the Slammers were reduced to such primitive techniques. Each phaseline was drawn across a particular landmark, normally a town, and was used to let Bull know where his sub-elements were located.

"While we may have to alter our route as we go, I propose that we take this route: Madden to Lakeside, then to Glendale, Cullea, and Nickel Run. That's where the mountains start. We'll turn right at the second fork after Nickel Run, left at the first tee junction, then right at the second tee, into Regarra and on to the wreck itself. That's when the job'll really begin . . . Sergeant Major Ogren's job. The phaselines, in order, are labeled Indigo, Fawn, Lavender, Rust—that's Nickel Run—Blue, Brown, White, Gold, and Iridium—that's our Slammers."

"Iridium," one of the new lieutenants murmured appreciatively.

"That's our goal," Bull agreed. "We can't stop for anyone. We've got to open that road. Any questions?"

"What formation are we using, sir?" Lieutenant Dyer of Foxtrot Alpha Tango inquired.

Bull pursed his lips. He hadn't decided on a formation yet. Although he would be able to change it as the need arose, he would still pay the penalty if the chosen formation didn't suit the terrain if they were attacked. There were some mountains on the west side of their route out to Cullea, particularly one near Glendale. The rest of the terrain was fairly flat. Still, Bull thought that the only two formations he would choose would be a tank shield with the skimmers in close behind his panzers, or a skimmer recon with a tank back up.

If Bull chooses the tank-shield formation, turn to section 26.

If he chooses the skimmer recon formation, turn to section 28.

— 18 —

Going north to the Crag Mountains and the Crageen was too risky. A single man armed with dynamite could make the roads impassable to softskinned vehicles that relied on wheels. Bull also felt that the central route, going northwest, was far too likely a route. The enemy would expect him to go that way. No, the lower route, going west first, then north to the wreck made more sense. He would have some cover from the forests and maybe some trouble, but the rest of the route was perfect. Bull started to tell Ennis his decision when he noticed that the young corporal was watching him intently. A slow smile played across Bull's lips. He would see just what kind of a gambler Corporal James K. Ennis really was.

"Did you bet on this one, Keith?" Bull asked the corporal, using his favored middle name.

"Me? Bet?" Ennis exclaimed in mock innocence.

"I hope you put your money on the lower route, through the forests," Bull told him.

"Damn!"

"How much did you lose?" Bull inquired.

"Fifty credits!" Ennis replied. "I was certain that you'd take the central route straight through."

"Make that one hundred credits," Bull said. "You know what I said."

"You didn't say anything about gambling, sir!" Ennis complained.

"No," Bull agreed. "I said that the next time you were wrong, it'd cost you." His corporal sighed. "You can pay me later," Bull told him. "Now, did you make up the overlays for the lower route, or were you wrong twice?"

"No sir!" Ennis replied, displaying the roll of overlays in his right hand.

"That's good. My officers will be relieved." Out of the corner of his eye Bull noted that those officers had arrived. He shouted down to them, "Ah, gentlemen! I'm glad to see you're prompt."

Lieutenant Dyer smiled, knowing that Bull was joking with them. "Ready when you are, sir!" Dyer told him.

"At least, we'll be ready as soon as you tell us where we're going, sir." Lieutenant Peyton amended.

"We're taking the lower route: first west, then north," Bull told them. "It's unlikely that we'll meet any resistance on that route, but if we do, the infantry section of this combat team—correction, this combat group—will be well able to neutralize it. Jebbitt and his men never did understand that tankers could let you pongoes do some work from time to time."

Lieutenant Peyton groaned. His feet were still recovering from the last maneuvers of the war. A skimmer could carry a man to a battle, but when it finally came to it, an infantryman fought on his feet.

"Never fear, Sergeant . . . uh, Lieutenant Peyton," Bull reassured him. "I am going to do my best to avoid making you work." His tone became more serious. "As you know, we're going to clear the way for Sergeant Major Ogren and the relief column in the softskinned vehicles. Our Slammers are dying out there, gentlemen. Now, if you'll look at your overlays, you'll see that our route is left at the first tee junction, at Plains, then a jog south to Smithtown and a wide arc north to Tooey, Regarra, and finally the wreck itself. Starting with the junction, those are phaselines Orange, Aqua, Red, Amber, Gold, and Iridium respectively. If we have to, we can switch to the central plains route at any of several points along the route. Let's get going."

While his officers gathered up their gear, Lieutenant Bromley looked at the overlays again. Slammers did not normally use phaselines, relying on instant computer displays to show the locations of all known enemy and friendly troops. Phaselines had been used extensively in the twentieth century by commanders not so equipped, to keep track of the progress of their sub-elements. Without the satellites to spot for them, the Slammers were reduced to such primitive techniques. Each phaseline was drawn across a particular landmark, normally a town, and was used to let Bull know where his sub-elements were located.

"A question, sir," Sergeant Beirne said. "What formation are we going to use?"

Lieutenant Bromley hadn't yet decided which of two possible formations he was going to use. The open terrain suggested either skimmer recon with hovertank follow-up, or the hovertank shield formation. The danger of using skimmers for recon was that they were scantily armored and easily neutralized if surprised at a distance from the tanks. But the stealth and maneuverability of the skimmers gave them the ability to travel almost unnoticed. Choosing the tank shield formation would protect his valuable skimmers but not give them the capability of searching out potential ambushes.

If Bull chooses to use skimmer recon, turn to section 23.

If Bull opts for the tank shield formation, turn to section 24.

— 19 —

"The tanks will go first," Bull told them. "Skimmers will follow up tight behind. And further questions?" He paused. "Good. We'll move out in five minutes. The formation will be the platoon wedge. My platoon will form the left side, Foxtrot Alpha Tango will take the right. The infantry will follow up in a three-platoon wedge. Lieutenant Smyth's platoon will be in the van, Alpha and Bravo on the left and right. If there's any difficulty, Alpha and Bravo will hold position to form a defensive screen for the softskinned vehicles. The two tank platoons will engage fire and move with Lieutenant Smyth's platoon, supporting as required. Is that clear?" Bull engaged the eyes of each lieutenant in turn. They all nodded. "Very well, let's move."

As the lieutenants dispersed, Bull climbed into his hovertank and readjusted his navigation display. With practiced fingers he adjusted his helmet and positioned the boom mike.

"Fire up the fans, Timmons," he told his driver. "Ennis, how's our ammo?"

"Fully loaded, sir," Corporal Ennis replied in a tone that indicated just a little bit of hurt that his lieutenant would have to ask.

"Very good." To his comm chief he said, "How about it, Sara?"

"Not so good, sir," Sara Engles replied. "Central control says that we're going to be out of contact with them almost immediately. As for the rest of the group, we'll have no problem."

"Very good. Give me the platoon push," Bull told her. "Lariat Two this is Lariat Two Six, report."

The throaty voice of Sergeant Lewis was the first back to him. "Two Zero," Lewis said.

"Two Eight," Sergeant Gleeson reported.

"Two Four," Sergeant Healey responded, finishing the roll.

"Roger," Bull agreed. "Prepare to move on my orders. We will form the lest flank of the wedge, standard formation." He continued to the combat group, knowing that Sara Engles would switch frequencies for him, "Foxtrot, this is Foxtrot Six. Report."

"Foxtrot Alpha Tango, ready," Lieutenant Dyer reported.

"Foxtrot India, ready," Smyth told him.

"Foxtrot Alpha India, ready," Lieutenant Peyton replied.

"Foxtrot Bravo India, ready and awaiting orders," Bravo's platoon leader responded.

Bull poked his head out of the hatch and brought his command seat up under him. With a look around, he saw that all of his force was hovering on their fans. Behind them he could see the mass of trucks and other softskinned vehicles that Operations had hastily collected. Inside the tank Engles was examining her radios, ready to outguess her commander yet again. Ennis had his head out the other hatch, peering forward and then backward with an occasion surreptitious glance at his commander. Bull glanced down at the vision blocks inside the turret and adjusted one for three sixty display. Then he made sure that his foot was safely away from the main gun's pedal trigger and that the big gun was loaded and ready. The fat safety glowed red; the great two-hundred-millimeter gun was ready to deal death.

"Central, this is Foxtrot. Prepared to move. Over," Bull reported to Central.

"This is Central." Colonel Hammer's rasp made it all too plain exactly who it was. "Move out."

"Roger. Out," Bull replied. To his combat group he said, "Foxtrot this is Foxtrot Six, move out." To his driver he said: "Roll it!"

"Righto, sir!" His driver was drowned out by the platoon responding as if in one voice: "This is Foxtrot Alpha Tango, roger. Foxtrot India, roger. Foxtrot Alpha India, Roger. Foxtrot Bravo India, roger." Above the radio traffic the huge roar of eight hovertank fans and the smaller skimmer fans of twelve infantry squads beat the air.

Combat Group Foxtrot moved out of the compound. As expected, Dyer's tank platoon took the road to the right while Bull's tank platoon took the road to the left. Outside of town they regrouped again on the main road, his platoon on the left and the other on the right. Bull decided that Lieutenant Dyer was doing all right. He swiveled to look behind him and saw the infantry skimmers fanned out in proper order. In training or not, Bull decided, those three platoons were doing all right. Further behind them, the softskinned vehicles were tearing down the road. The weather was sunny and clear.

They reached the junction in ten minutes. Off to the right Bromley could distinguish a forest. To the left were open fields and the road that led to Plains. The combat group turned left.

"Foxtrot Tango, Foxtrot Alpha Tango, increase your dispersion to two hundred meters. Keep you eyes open," Bull said over the combat-group frequency. With such a gap he would have coverage eight hundred meters to either side of the road. It made him edgy not to have better coverage, but he didn't want his tanks to lose sight of each other.

"Roger," Lieutenant Dyer of Alpha Tango replied.

The march from the junction to Plains eased Bull's misgivings somewhat. There were several motorists on the road, showing signs of alarm at the movements of his forces, but that was reassuring. If the motorists weren't there or looked relieved, it would indicate to Bull that something was wrong.

Outside of Plains he ordered the two outermost sections of the tank platoons to perform a pincer recon around the outskirts of the town. They reported nothing out of the ordinary. Relieved, Bull moved the rest of his tanks through the village. Townspeople quickly cleared the streets. Some appeared very apprehensive. Perhaps they feared that the Slammers would repeat the atrocities of the Raiders. The thought upset Bull, but it was clear to him that common folk would never understand what drove a man to become a mercenary or what kept him in the trade.

The memory came into Bull's mind unbidden. Murea had been a lovely planet, and he had been born to riches. He was Braddington Paul Bromley, the fourth of that name. Early on he had been trained in the martial arts and military skill.

Murea was peaceful but it had not always been so. It was his honor to join the armed forces of his planet, as a commissioned officer, of course.

Murea decided it was her honor to aid the ruling class of Artair, a planet in another solar system, and so off Bull had gone. He was soon disillusioned, of the war and of the people he was fighting for. On Murea his ruling class had put the welfare of the people above their own welfare. On Artair the ruling class crushed, and he found himself fighting on the side of the crushers. Worse, they fought badly. When his Murean men died in the many skirmishes of the war, they were replaced by half-trained recruits from Artair itself. These were sullen and poor fighters drafted from the middle and lower classes. Even so, Bull upheld his honor and trained his new men to fight as best they could. His unit was not armored, but consisted of several very old armored personnel carriers and a few wheeled jeeps. Still, Bull's Bucks did themselves proud in combat—until they faced the mercenary regiment of Colonel Alois Hammer.

Bull's Bucks fought three engagements with the Slammers and gave ground in each. Against the might of hovertanks, combat cars, and satellite-guided artillery, there was nothing Bull could do. He had no weaponry that could penetrate the armor of a hovertank, and the smallest powergun went through his armored cars like a knife through butter. He was captured as his force disintegrated in the fire of the third engagement. Not that two APC's and a few ground troops could be called a force. The Slammers treated him well enough. As a gentleman of honor, he was allowed parole in the confinement area.

It was there he had found out that his home world had pulled out of the war, disgusted by the very people it had sent aid to succor. Having changed its mind, Murea wanted no reminders of its mistake. Murea refused to ransom him back. As the war closed, with victory going to the Slammers, Bull found himself without the means to buy passage home. The new government of Artair bore him no ill will and released him to do as he pleased. He had no money to contact his kin and no way to tell them that he was still alive. With a firm resolve, he had walked from the exit of the confinement barracks to the enlistment office of Hammer's regiment.

"Lieutenant." The voice of Sara Engles brought him back to the present.

"What is it?" he asked.

"Sergeant Lewis, sir."

"Go ahead, Sam," Bull said to his platoon sergeant.

"I don't know if it's important, sir, but I caught a glint from that hill to the southwest of us," Sam Lewis told him.

"Sounds about right," Bull agreed. It made sense. Now he knew why he'd been thinking back to Murea. That mountain was a perfect place to hide some tanks. They would have an excellent chance to fire on the plains, maybe three full salvos before the powerguns of his panzers could level the mountain. Maybe more. "How many, do you know?" Bull asked.

"I'm on IR and I can't count 'em yet," Lewis replied.

Bull thought, if infrared couldn't detect the tanks, they must have had their engines off for a while or they'd taken good hull-down positions. But even hull down, the heat from their exhausts would give them away, which meant that they must have their engines off. The Raiders, though not very good tankers, knew that Bull's powerguns would get them unless they could move after every shot. It bothered Bull that they would take such a chance.

"Sara, send Central a spot report and put me on Tango Alpha's push." As soon as Bull heard the squawk that indicated his frequency had changed, he said, "Dyer, check your area. We've got a spot report over here."

"Roger," Dyer replied calmly. "You heard the man, take a good look around," he said to his platoon.

On a lower level Bull heard his communications chief relaying the spot report to Central and Central noting it calmly.

"Sergeant Hopkins here, sir." The voice boomed in Bull's helmet. "I think I see something in the forest ahead."

"Sara, Sergeant Major!" Bull ordered. "Ogren, ground!"

"Roger," Sergeant Major Ogren replied. "All vehicles off road."

"Foxtrot this is Foxtrot Six," Bull told his combat group. "We have two enemy positions ahead: one on the mountain to the southwest, the other in the forest to the north. Foxtrot Tango and Foxtrot Alpha India will engage to the west. Foxtrot Alpha Tango and Foxtrot Bravo India will engage to the north. Foxtrot India will ground in Plains and render assistance as required to the softskinneds."

"Alpha India, roger."

"Alpha Tango, roger."

"Bravo India, roger."

"Foxtrot India, wilco," Smyth finished the acknowledgments.

"You skimmers make sure you stick close by the tanks," Bull told them. "Move out!"

Bull's tank and the other tank in his section, Lariat Two Eight, started toward the mountain with a squad of skimmers behind each hovertank. Without having to be told, Timmons grounded the huge panzer after they had come a kilometer. Behind him and over his helmet speakers, Bull could hear Sergeant Lewis and the other tank section roaring along to leapfrog beyond him. Four bolts flashed from the mountain to land in front of him. When he could see again, he saw that Lewis's tank had taken a glancing blow but was gamely moving on, a bright streak showing where part of its armor had been melted.

"Foxtrot, this is Alpha Tango," Dyer reported. "We are engaging two tanks in the forest."

"Roger." Bull acknowledged. "We've got four here."

The enemy has a total of six tanks, four on the mountain and two in the forest. Their firepower is being combined and they are well hidden. Each tank has an Ordnance value of 2.

Lieutenant Bromley's forces consist of eight hovertanks and twelve squads of skimmers, including Lieutenant Smyth's platoon's supporting fire. The Ordnance value of Bull's panzers is 4 each while each skimmer infantry squad has an Ordnance value of 2. Total the two atack values, and alternate casualties.

The enemy will exchange no more than three volleys with Group Foxtrot, then withdraw. The enemy uses Chart C, while the Slammers use Chart B.

If the enemy is destroyed or driven off, turn to section 25.

If the enemy succeeds in destroying Group Foxtrot, turn to section 29.

— 20 —

"The tanks will form a recon wedge with the infantry to follow up," Bull decided. "That will expose those forces best able to take punishment to any enemy and protect the infantry skimmers, which are better for rapid stealthy movement." The two younger infantry officers exchanged disgusted looks, but Bull only grinned. "You'll see enough action if this gets rough," he told them, "and if it doesn't, then training will make up for it."

"Then you don't think there's much danger, sir?" the newly appointed platoon leader of Foxtrot Bravo India inquired.

"Just civilians being foolish," Bull replied. "We'll slice through and scatter them when we find 'em." He only partly believed what he said; mostly he said it to stiffen the resolve of these untried leaders. The trick was to move, and quickly, Bull realized. "Any more questions? Good. Move out in five minutes." He swung himself up to the turret, dismissing the officers.

"What's my callsign?" Ogren growled at him as the others turned away.

"Sierra Major," Bull replied instantly, and then decided to stick with it. "It suits."

Ogren grunted and stared at Bull's retreating back for a moment before he moved off to organize his ragged command.

Bull clambered up into the turret of the huge hovertank. Inside, he grabbed his combat helmet and pulled it on, ensuring that the boom mike was just in front of his lips and that the helmet was on tight enough to cut out the roar of the tank's huge fans.

"Fire it up, Timmons!" Bull told his driver. Immediately, the huge tank quivered with the surge of energy as Timmons powered up the huge lift fans. Of his radio chief Bull asked, "How're the sets, Sara?"

The muttered invective with a "sir" thrown in for luck convinced Bull that his laserlink radios were in good condition. It wasn't just Engles's ability to scrounge radio gear that made her invaluable. She seemed to be able to second guess Bull's needs; never, in months of fighting, had he needed to ask her to switch frequencies for him as he swapped between platoon, company, battalion, and regimental frequencies.

"Lariat Two," Bull said over the platoon net, using his platoon's official designation as second platoon, L Company.

"Two Zero, ready," Sergeant Lewis's assured voice rasped.

"Two Four." "Two Eight," Sergeant's Healey and Gleeson replied, echoing that they, too, were ready to move out.

On the group communications net he said, "Foxtrot, report."

"Foxtrot Alpha Tango, ready."

"Foxtrot Alpha India, ready."

"Foxtrot India, ready."

"Foxtrot Bravo India, ready."

"Sierra Major, ready," Sergeant Major Ogren said, completing the roll call.

"Central, this is Foxtrot Six, prepared to move," Bull informed Central on still another net.

"Move out!" the gruff voice of Alois Hammer told him.

"Foxtrot, move out!" Bull told his command. Immediately his tank surged forward as Timmons angled the fans. Behind him seven more tanks and twelve squads of skimmer-mounted infantry did likewise. Farther back the wheeled softskinned vehicles fed power through their transmissions and growled forward, picking up speed as the hovercraft in front of them surged ahead.

The small task force left the compound and the town which surrounded it behind them. In less than ten minutes they were at phaseline Yellow, the tee junction where they turned left. They passed by a forest off to their right and fields full of farmers on their left as the combat group headed on toward the town of Plains, phaseline Aqua. The weather was fair and sunny with good visibility. Bull began to feel that maybe what he had told Bravo India's platoon leader was true, that the survivors of the downed transport were being harried by a few disgruntled civilians who would scatter in the face of armed, organized troops.

All the same, I shouldn't set a bad example, Bull thought to himself. He pulled out his binoculars and scanned the terrain leading up to Plains. In the fields, farmers worked. In the town, people appeared to be going about their business. Beyond Plains to the southwest was a large hill, an outcast from the great Crags to the north. Gorse and a few trees dotted it. Nothing in his view pricked his conscience or raised hairs on the back of his neck. He wasn't too surprised; this was far too close to the Slammer's compound. Most of the Slammers might be gone, but even the cowardly remnants of Jebbitt's Raiders, huddling somewhere out in the Crags, knew better than to tackle those Slammers who remained.

"Foxtrot, this is Six. Secure Aqua," Bull ordered. To his driver he said, "Move it, Greg! I want to be out of there first."

"Should I recon?" Sam Lewis asked, trying to drop the hint.

"Negative," Bull replied. "There's no need."

The combat group bottled up as it roared through the small town of Plains, the great tanks swerving through the crooked streets which had not long ago been cow paths. Behind them the softskinned vehicles bundled together and slowed down.

"Move it! Move it!" Bull roared to his command, frustrated with the way things were going. "Foxtrot India, get it together!" Bull said to Smyth, singling him out. Bull felt he had to keep pushing his command, force them to move at the same speed they had used when outmaneuvering Jebbitt's Raiders— speed which through the millennia had been called Caesar speed, blitzkrieg, and finally "Bull speed."

"Bull speed it is, sir!" Timmons replied, squeezing the last watt of power out of the immense fusion reactor that powered their tank. Behind them the rest of Bull's platoon began to fan out to their left to form half of the wedge formation maintained by the hovertanks. Lieutenant Dyer's tank platoon followed up shortly but had trouble linking up with Bull, since they were far behind.

"Foxtrot Six this is Foxtrot Alpha Tango. Request reduced speed to regroup," Dyer was finally forced to say.

"Negative," Bull replied. The time for worrying about formation was later, when they were nearer the wreck. Speed was what counted. Farther back the skimmers were forming up just outside of Plains, in keeping with the general formation Bull had prescribed. Things were going well enough, Bull decided, and if there really was going to be trouble, it wouldn't help the survivors of the wreck if they arrived too late.

Unwillingly, Bull remembered the only time he had arrived too late. He had been born Braddington Paul Bromley on his home planet of Murea, and was the fourth to bear that name. His family had been part of the planet's enlightened rich, and ruled with a wise hand. As was fitting a man of his standing, he was trained early on in the martial arts and military science, even though Murea was a united, peaceful planet. It was his misfortune that, while he was serving with the elite guard of Murea, the politicians decided to aid the aristocracy of Artair, a distant planet circling another sun. Bull fought well, but the Murean detachment was the only good unit on the side of the aristocracy, and shortly they were defeated. The victors, mindful of repercussions, treated the captured Mureans well and returned them to their home planet.

Murea was not the same when Bull returned. The politicians who had unwisely sent aid to Artair had also antagonized a large faction of their own populace. Taking note of the successful revolution of the Artairians, the disgruntled lower classes decided to emulate them.

The rebellion erupted quickly. Bull was put back into uniform in charge of troops drafted from the same segment of the population they were supposed to control. Bull and every other officer found themselves more nervous in front of their own troops than in front of the enemy. As the situation worsened and droves of trained regular troops deserted to the enemy over the bodies of their officers, Hammers' Slammers were hired.

The Slammers swiftly crushed the rebels in a series of lightning moves that tantalized young Braddington Bromley. With those remnants of his command who stood by him, he emulated their actions, earning quite a reputation among his own men. Unlike the well-equipped Slammers, Bromley did not possess the satellite tracking systems and the assistance of ever-present Central, so his ripostes were made swiftly but with caution. He never began a movement without first ensuring that his formation was properly established and his men well rested. It was in the midst of one of these rapid ripostes against the rebels that Bull found the remains of his ancestral home. The fire was still burning, blood still oozing out of the bodies of his parents. He had taken time before cresting the hill in front of his home, to regroup so that his unit was properly arrayed for battle. While he had been ordering his unit, the enemy had been murdering his family.

When the war ended, he had nothing left worth going back to. He had entered the recruiting shack of Alois Hammer's regiment in the full Murean parade dress of a lieutenant colonel. He had left in the drab clothing of a Slammer private.

A bolt of light followed by a loud explosion rocked Bull back to the present. Two Six lurched to the side as Timmons tried to recover the huge blower from a near hit.

"Bloody hell!" Ennis exclaimed. "It came from the forest!" he said, pointing to the trees north of them. Another bolt roared over their heads. "That was from the hill behind us!"

"Ambush!" Dyer yelled over the combat group net. Numbly, Bull took in the situation. An unknown number of tanks were hidden in the forest to the north and the hill to the southwest. His tanks were strewn out on the open plains while his skimmers were still emerging from the town.

Bull shook himself to action, delaying recrimination for a more suitable time. "Skimmers ground!" Bull yelled, hoping they still hadn't cleared the town. "All tanks proceed toward the forest," he continued. "Foxtrot Tango, target the hill. Alpha Tango target the forest. Skimmers support as targets become available. Do it now!"

"Roger," Dyer replied in a tight voice.

"Wilco," Smyth acknowledged for the skimmers.

Another bolt tore across the horizen toward Bull's tank. Cursing, Timmons swerved the huge panzer.

There are four enemy tanks on the hill to the southwest and two tanks in the forest to the north. Each tank has an Ordnance value of 2. They exchange three volleys with the Slammers before they retreat. The Slammers have eight tanks with an Ordinance value of 4.

Both the Slammers and their enemy fight using Chart C.

If the enemy is destroyed or driven off, turn to section 25.

If the Slammers are eliminated, turn to section 29.

— 21 —

The skimmers could flit in to the survivors of the wreck and talk to them, calm them down, and secure a path for Bull's tanks. It made sense, even if it didn't feel good.

"Do it," Bull agreed. "November, Gulf, stand fast."

Around him the skimmers flitted silently off toward the wreckage. "Be ready to aid and engage," he added to the disgruntled tankers.

"We do the work, they get the honor," Dyer grumbled.

Flickers of cyan and blue-green light told Bull that his comrades were engaged in mixed fighting, the sort his tanks could do little to aid. He peered through his binoculars and searched the terrain. The wreck had fallen more to one side than the other, Bull saw. He realized that it must have landed on its tail and rolled to the right a bit as it failed to make an emergency landing. Lighter, more scattered wreckage to the left led him to believe that side had been sabotaged. Something moved over there!

Something vaguely familiar.

"Ennis, come up here," Bull called to his corporal. "Timmons, get out of that seat; we're going scouting."

"What?" Ennis exclaimed.

"You cover us," Bull ordered, unhooking his helmet from the comlink and hoisting up his sidearm. In front of him Timmons scrambled out of the driver's seat and pulled his own gun free.

"Ready to go, boss!" Timmons called brightly.

"Quietly," Bull reminded him. "I thought I saw something over there in the glen."

Moving away from the tanks, which dropped from view in a surprisingly short time, Bull found himself nervous and more hesitant. The tanker in him felt bare and vulnerable, like a turtle out of its shell, but the Slammer in him was curious enough to go on foot where his tank would announce his presence too soon. Suddenly he heard talk. Waving a hand to Timmons, Bull crouched down.

The voices came from a rag tag camp hidden among the trees. One of them was slick and oily. Bull had heard it only once before, but he knew the name instantly. A look back at Timmons told him that the driver, too, grasped the importance of their discovery. With deft hand signals learned from the clever Pete Smyth, Bull and Timmons moved around to two corners of their targets' position.

"They broke through, I'm telling you!" a voice was explaining. "They're here!"

"If they're here, where are their tanks?" the oily voice replied. "It's only a few skimmers, nothing to worry about," the voice added soothingly. "We'll soon have the rest of the tanks in our hands, and then we'll be able to destroy these scum and move on to Hammer's base!" There was triumph and gloating victory in the voice.

"I wouldn't say so, Colonel Jebbitt," Bull called out softly.

"What! Who's out there?" Two shots rang toward Bull's position, but he was no longer there. From his new position several yards to the right, Bull could see the dull gleam of Timmons's weapon as he held the enemy in his sights.

"Lieutenant Braddington Bromley, commander, Combat Group Foxtrot," Bull replied, after rolling away from another volley of shots. "I'm here for your surrender."

"Foxtrot!" Jebbitt snarled.

"Migod!" the other man hissed.

"Surrender, Colonel. You've got nothing left," Bull said.

"Hah! I've got your stinking regiment wiped out," Jebbitt jeered. "*You* surrender."

Distracted by the conversation, Bull was surprised when a horde of ragged infantry rushed past Timmons's position toward Jebbitt.

"Don't shoot, Greg!" Bull warned when he recognized the pongoes as those who had been aboard the wrecked transport.

The fracas was short and sharp. Jebbitt was struck over the head by one of the men. "Foxtrot," Bull identified himself to the group as he walked forward with his sidearm slung over his shoulder.

"Foxtrot?" one of the dirtied Slammers exclaimed. "Via, it is! Sergeant John Green, sir!" The man came to rigid attention and snapped off a precise salute. "Glad to see you!"

"Come out, Timmons," Bull called. From the forest beyond, Greg Timmons pulled himself out of his camouflage, to the surprise and amazement of the infantry who had just rushed Jebbitt's camp.

In the clearing Bull could see that there were only two of the enemy: Jebbitt and his aide. They looked weary, torn, and beaten. In spite of the lump on his head, Jebbitt rose to his feet, straightened his back, and proclaimed, "I demand to be treated according to the articles of war!"

He was struck in the back by a suspicious pongo. "Yeah, right," the man said to the fallen colonel. He raised his rifle butt for another blow, but Bull kicked the weapon away. A wild expression crossed the man's eyes, but then he looked away.

"You'll be tried," Bull said tightly, thinking of the plains of Tegara and the crags of Kiltoween. "You'll be tried by the gun!" As Bull raised his weapon to fire, a bolt pierced Jebbitt through the chest and burned it clean out.

"You!" Jebbitt whispered, staring into Bull's eyes. Then he arched his back and sagged into a crumpled mass of burnt flesh, the sightless eyes still fixed on Bull Bromley's face.

Bull couldn't see where the shot had come from. Through clenched teeth he said, "The pleasure should have been mine."

Turn to section 137.

— 22 —

Pete Smyth was in the lead, where he belonged. He had longed for this moment, always longing to be in the front, to be at the point of first contact. Smyth could never quite figure out if it was because he wanted to know the worst before anyone else or just needed to be in the driver's seat.

He paused for a moment and scooted his skimmer into a small dip to look at the terrain in front of him. For a moment he cursed the fact that Colonel Hammer had already sent his jeeps off planet. The extra firepower and increased mobility would have been of incalculable aid. But the rest of the Slammers had taken heavy losses in jeeps, and Smyth's platoon could afford to do without while they were on training duty. Training duty! Smyth snorted.

And Bromley, going after his girl like that. Smyth had met Donna Mills when the Slammers had first touched down on Maffren. He'd helped her find a place for her parents to live after Jebbitt's Raiders had burned them out of their farm. But Bull had to have it all. It wasn't enough that he drive them all harder than any devil could dream; Bromley had to steal his woman, too.

A huge roar, instantly augmented by the smell of burnt air and a flash of blinding light, told Pete Smyth that he had not been careful enough.

"Report!" Bromley demanded brusquely. Just then another round of fire burst from the town. At least Smyth knew what was there—skimmers, probably a platoon. But where had that other, heavier, fire come from? Via, Smyth swore, have they got artillery?

The enemy has one platoon of skimmer-mounted infantry in the village and one hovertank-equipped platoon in the forest that straddles the road.

The four skimmers each have an Ordnance value of 2, and the four hovertanks each have an Ordnance value of 4. They have surprised the Slammers and attack using Chart B. The enemy withdraws after three rounds of combat. Total the combat values and alternate losses.

The Slammers are surprised and fight using Chart E.

If the Slammers are destroyed, turn to section 29.

If the enemy withdraws or is destroyed, turn to section 96.

— 23 —

Bull was convinced it would be foolish not to let his skimmers go first and recon the area. Forests were great places for a man with a buzzbomb to set up and catch a tank unaware. Considering how green some of his men were, Bull felt it would be best to give the pongoes a chance to settle their nerves before they were called upon to do real work.

"The infantry goes first," Bull decided. "I'd have to send you forward through the forests anyway, and this'll give you officers a chance to work out any wrinkles before it's too late." The two new infantry officers exchanged glances. Bull smiled, remembering his first time fighting for the Slammers.

"Don't worry," he reassured them. "You'll have your own personal eight-barrel artillery battery to support you," meaning his tanks, of course.

He turned to Sergeant Major Ogren. "Your callsign will be

Sierra Major,'' Bull told him, realizing how appropriate a
sign it was for the leader of the softskinned vehicles. ''How
are your men equipped?''

''They got sidearms mostly, and a few of the twenty-
millimeter powerguns,'' Ogren told him. ''I don't want to
lead them in a fight, Lieutenant. They'll have a hard enough
time when we finally get to the crash site.'' He snorted.
''Half of them are medics, and I've even got some civilian
doctors who volunteered to help out.''

Bull nodded. The situation was just about how he'd pic-
tured it. ''We'll make sure that the hardest work your people
have to do is splint some fractures at the wreck,'' Bull vowed.

''Lieutenant Smyth,'' Bull continued, looking his ex-cellmate
in the eye, ''your platoon will take point. Alpha will take the
left flank and Bravo the right.'' To Lieutenant Dyer he said,
''Your platoon will provide support to the right flank; I'll take
the left flank.''

Dyer nodded. ''How many cases do you plan to lose, sir?''

Many years ago Bull had started a platoon tradition of
awarding a case of beer to any tank crew that destroyed an
enemy tank. It was a pleasant tradition that had occasionally
put him out of pocket money, but it was the sort of thing that
kept a platoon together. The newly promoted Lieutenant
Dyer had been a member of Bull's platoon until they had
defeated Jebbitt's Raiders.

''Not to you, Lieutenant,'' Bull told him. ''You now have
the awesome responsibility of deciding whether or not you
want to bear the burden of such a tradition in your own
platoon!''

Dyer groaned but stopped midway and smiled. ''Make you
a bet, sir. I'll bet my platoon'll destroy more of the enemy
than your platoon.''

''Done!'' Ennis cried from the observer's turret. Bull and
the other officers stared up at him in surprise. Ennis turned
bright red and stammered, ''I mean, sir, you should take him
up on the offer.''

''My corporal is right, Dyer,'' Bull agreed. ''I hope you
still have that bounty money you earned when we destroyed
Jebbitt's Raiders.'' Bull turned to address the gathered officers.
''Now, gentlemen, let's earn our wages. We move out in five
minutes.''

Bull jumped into the turret of his tank, grabbing up his

combat helmet in one fluid movement. Behind him the other officers hastened to their vehicles. Bull adjusted the boom mike on his helmet so that it was just in front of his lips, and tightened the chin strap so the noise of the blowers did not prevent him from hearing the radio. Inside the tank the other members of his crew hastened to complete final preparations. Sara Engles, his radio operator, finished her inspection of the four radios Lariat Two Six carried. Corporal Ennis adjusted his seat position so that he was exposed to the outside from the chest up and had a good grip on the twenty-millimeter machine gun the tank carried in the turret.

Far in front in another hatch, Greg Timmons waited, ready to feed power from the tank's fusion reactor to its four huge hover fans and lift the tank into action.

"Ready, Sara?" Bull inquired. She had magicked two extra radios from somewhere—Bull didn't want to know where—and quickly earned her reputation as a mind reader. Bull never had to tell her which frequency or "push" he wanted to communicate on. Sara always knew and switched before he started to say anything.

"You just talk, Lieutenant," she had told him in one of her rare moments of charity. "I'll do the rest." And she did. Many times her ability to second guess Bull had saved all their lives.

"Ready," she told him now. "Aren't you?"

Bull grimaced. It didn't matter that he was a lieutenant and outranked her, could dock her pay or even, in rare circumstances, get her thrown out of the Slammers. Sara Engles spoke to him as she did to everyone else, with the possible exception of a very rare "sir" thrown in from time to time.

"Foxtrot, this is Six," Bull said by way of reply. "Report."

"Foxtrot India, Alpha India, and Bravo India, awaiting orders," Pete Smyth replied, indicating that he had already assumed command of the infantry elements of Combat Group Foxtrot.

"Foxtrot Alpha Tango, ready," Lieutenant Dyer replied after a short pause to recover from Smyth's rapid-fire answer.

"Sierra Major, here. Let's move it," Ogren said from the rear.

"Central, this is Foxtrot, prepared to move. Over," Bull told Central on the regimental push.

"Get going!" the voice of Alois Hammer snarled back.

"Roger; out," Bull acknowledged. To his command he said, "Advance."

The soft whine of skimmers whizzed by him as the three infantry platoons took their forward positions, rushing out of the compound and into the city beyond. Bull noted that they herringboned their guns to the left and right as they moved into the city, trusting no one.

"Lariat, advance," Bull said to his own platoon after ensuring that all the infantry skimmers had left. Timmons poured power into the fans as soon as Bull had finished speaking. A short moment later he told Dyer, "Alpha Tango, advance."

"Roger," Dyer replied, the roar of fans coming with his transmission indicating that he had already started moving.

The huge tanks left the compound and gathered speed as they made their way from narrow city roads onto the main road leaving the city. Ahead of them the infantry skimmers had already spread out to either side of the road, nudging into nooks and crannies as they investigated potential trouble areas and reported them clear. Bull took his binoculars and peered ahead to the tee junction they were fast approaching, leaving the proper positioning of his tank to Ennis and of his platoon to Sam Lewis.

"Foxtrot, this is India. Orange secured," Pete Smyth reported shortly, indicating that he had reached the tee junction and found nothing out of the ordinary.

"Proceed to Aqua," Bull replied, telling Smyth to advance to the town of Plains. With his binoculars he could see Smyth's skimmers veer to the left as his platoon bracketed the road in its turn to the left. Farther out the other two infantry platoons made similar maneuvers. Bravo platoon had to really push it to make up the greater distance to travel, and Bull could see the infantrymen hanging on to their skimmers for dear life.

"Foxtrot, this is Foxtrot Bravo India," a young platoon leader radioed Bull. It was rare for an infantry leader to call on a tank leader, particularly the group leader.

"This is Foxtrot," Bull replied warily.

"Request permission to recon the forest to the northeast between Orange and Aqua," the platoon leader asked.

"Refer that request to Foxtrot India," Bull replied gruffly. If the silly fool didn't know who was running the forward recon, he'd soon find out. If he did know and was trying to go above Pete Smyth's head, he'd made a big mistake. Bull might be worried about Smyth, but when he gave a man a job, he didn't tie the man's hands.

"Permission denied," Smyth told Bravo India. "Again," he added with some venom.

To Sara, Bull said, "Put me on that young twerp's push!"

"You're already there," she told him in a bored tone.

"Uniform Two Six, this is Lariat Two Six," Bull growled. He wouldn't have his officers trying such tricks!

"Go ahead, over."

"You will adhere to orders issued by Foxtrot India until told otherwise by this command," Bull told the platoon leader forcefully. "Is that understood?"

"Roger," the young officer replied sheepishly.

"Lariat Two Six, out."

"Thanks," Pete Smyth said on Bull's platoon push.

"Nothing," Bull told him.

"I'd like to wheel under Aqua and let that young puppy secure it himself," Smyth told him. "It'd save us some time, and he could also set up road guards for Sierra."

"Go for it," Bull replied. With that change, the bulk of the skimmers would wheel southwest outside of Plains, leaving Bravo India to investigate and secure the town for the softskinned vehicles. The advantage would be that they wouldn't have a bottleneck as several infantry platoons and the two tank platoons tried to pour through the small village roads.

By way of reply, Smyth called over the radio, "Foxtrot Bravo India, secure Aqua. Foxtrot Alpha India, maintain relative position. We will pass under Aqua en route to Red. Foxtrot, request that Foxtrot Alpha Tango continue to provide support for Foxtrot Bravo India and Foxtrot Tango support all other India elements. Over."

"Bravo India, say again, over," the now nervous young lieutenant replied.

"I say again, secure Aqua. Over," Smyth responded calmly.

"Bravo India, wilco."

"Foxtrot Alpha Tango, wilco," Dyer added with a note of humor to his voice.

"Gotcha covered India," Bull told Smyth.

"Roger," Smyth concurred. "Foxtrot Bravo India, you are also required to provide assistance for the Sierra Major element in transit through Aqua. Over."

"Bravo India, roger." The voices of the young platoon leader sounded even less enthused than before.

"Never you fear, I'll look after you," Dyer chided him.

"Maintain proper radio discipline," Bull growled to everyone, especially Dyer. He was rewarded with a lengthy silence. "Ennis, mind the fort. I'm going to keep an eye on our young puppy."

"Yes sir," Corporal Ennis acknowledged, his tone indicating that he had kept himself informed of the goings-on in the various command networks.

In his binoculars Bull saw Bravo India's skimmers proceed into Plains. Behind them, moving more slowly, the huge tanks of Lieutenants Dyer's platoon waited to provide any aid required. Bull got an occasional glimpse of skimmers as they nudged around the outskirts of the town.

"Foxtrot India, this is Foxtrot India Bravo. Aqua is secured," the young officer told Smyth finally.

"Roger," Lieutenant Smyth acknowledged. Then to Bull he said, "Foxtrot Six this is Foxtrot India, request permission to proceed to phaseline Red."

"This is Six; go for it," Bull told him. "Foxtrot, proceed to phaseline Red," he said to the rest of his command.

Combat Group Foxtrot wheeled to the southwest, Lieutenant Smyth's platoon widening its dispersion to cover for Bravo India, which was providing security at Plains for the softskinned vehicles. Lieutenant Dyer moved his platoon forward so that it was to the west of Plains in anticipation of Bravo India's move out of the town and back into the standard formation. Bull's platoon maintained a position on the left of the road, covering both Smyth's and Peyton's skimmers. Things were going smoothly.

Dyer's voice broke the calm: "Foxtrot this is Alpha Tango. I've got a contact in the forest to the north of Aqua. I've got another contact on the hill to the west of Aqua. Four enemy tanks on the hill!!" His voice was no longer calm.

"This is Foxtrot. All units engage!" Bull roared, but his voice was drowned out by a shell exploding just in front of them. Timmons swerved the huge tank sharply to the right, slamming Bull against the hatch coaming. Two more shells burst to their left, just where the tank had been seconds before. In front of him smoke was rising from several other shell hits. To his right he could see the explosions as shells from the tanks in the forest rained into Plains.

"Dyer! Attack those units in the forest!" Bull ordered. "Bravo India, provide cover fire!" To the rest of his command he said, "India and Alpha India, cover and fire to the hill. We'll cover for you!"

There are four enemy tanks on the hill to the west of Plains and two enemy tanks in the forest to the north of Plains. Each enemy tank has an Ordnance value of 2.

Bull's Combat Group Foxtrot has eight hovertanks with an Ordance value of 4, and twelve skimmer squads each with an Ordnance value of 2. Total the attack strengths and alternate losses.

The enemy exchanges no more than three volleys before withdrawing. Both the enemy and the Slammers attack using Chart C.

If the enemy is destroyed or withdraws, turn to section 27.

If the enemy destroys Combat Group Foxtrot, turn to section 29.

— 24 —

He made the decision instantly. "Our hovertanks will go first, at least as far as the forest. Then we'll see." He looked at the newly promoted Lieutenant Dyer. "Your platoon will have the right flank, mine will take the left. Lieutenant Peyton's platoon will snuggle up in your wake." Peyton made a face. "You don't have to get too close," Bull told him, "just close enough to get dirt in your face." To the leader of the other training infantry platoon Bull said, "Your platoon has the honor of eating my dust." The young man grinned.

Bull locked eyes with Lieutenant Smyth. "For the time being your job will be to form the van for the softskinned vehicles." He looked over to Sergeant Major Ogren. "I suppose you know what to do?"

Ogren snorted. "You open the door, we'll close it. Just you open the door . . ." He paused, then added, "sir."

Bull nodded. He wondered how he'd had the luck to get the sergeant major leading the softskinned vehicles, until he recalled that Colonel Hammer had assigned him. Maybe it wasn't so much a matter of luck after all. Sergeant Major Ogren had been known to force obedience in the worst of situations.

"We leave in five minutes. I'll contact you by laserlink," Bull finished, climbing back into his turret. He watched as the officers headed back to their commands, and then fastened his helmet. With a deft motion he adjusted the boom mike hanging from his helmet to just in front of his lips and tightened up the chin strap so that outside noise was cut off. A quick glance told him that the great two-hundred-millimeter main gun was armed and ready, while a caress was all Bull needed to know that the two-centimeter turret gun was yearning for action.

"Fire it up, Timmons," Bull said over the intercom. To his corporal he said, "I hope you didn't bet we wouldn't need any ammo!"

"No sir! We're fully combat loaded," Corporal Ennis replied. "It took us three minutes to switch from training to combat ammo. That's a new battalion record."

"Sar' Major," Sara Engles muttered. She was the fourth member of the crew, Bromley's communications chief. She had joined his tank when he'd made first lieutenant, and had instantly displayed a talent close to mind reading. She always had the radios switched to whatever frequency Bromley needed before he could ask. She was taciturn, stalwart, and stubborn; Bull would never trade her.

"She's right. Sergeant Major Ogren sort of helped," Ennis agreed.

"Have you briefed Timmons on the route?" Bull asked.

"Yes sir, he showed me the way," Timmons replied. "I'll get you there as quick as you want. Just let me dodge the trees." On their last mission Bull had ordered his driver to topple trees to hinder the movement of Jebbitt's ground tanks. Timmons had complained mightily about the delay and lost time.

"I'm not trying to slow anyone down this time," Bull responded. "Get ready," he said to his crew in general. "Foxtrot this is Foxtrot Six, report," Bull said over the radio. He could never figure out how it was that Engles always knew which channel to switch to before he said anything, but she did, and it had saved their lives several times.

"Foxtrot Alpha Tango." Dyer's terse reply indicated that he was ready to move out.

"Foxtrot Alpha India." Lieutenant Peyton's reply was a scant moment behind.

"Foxtrot Bravo India, wait one. Over," a young voice Bull didn't recognize replied. Shortly afterward Bull heard "Foxtrot Bravo India" from the platoon leader.

"This is Foxtrot India, roger," Smyth responded in a bored tone that seemed to say "What took you so long?"

"Sierra Major, waiting impatiently," Ogren grumped.

Good, Bull thought to himself. Now for Central. "Central, this is Foxtrot. Moving at this time."

"Roger," the voice of Central replied calmly.

"Foxtrot, move out," Bull told his command. Instantly he felt the surge of power as Timmons changed the thrust of the fans and the huge tank glided forward. Behind him the sound of seven more hovertanks filled the air. Farther behind the soft noise of skimmers made no appreciable difference, though the heavy engines of the softskinned, wheeled vehicles that had been hastily rounded up by the regiment added another tone.

The tanks cleared the gate and instantly assumed a column separation of fifty meters, guns hedgehogged left and right to cover either side of the wide streets of Madden. Behind them, with less trepidation, rode the infantry on their skimmers. The huge panzers slid slightly around the tight corners that Timmons's blistering pace encouraged, and scraped the tanks' rusty hover skirts against the road, raising sparks. Finally they cleared the town on a wide but poorly paved road.

Bull's platoon fanned out to the left and Lieutenant Dyer's tank platoon fanned out to the right. Together they formed a wedge behind which the two infantry platoons arrayed themselves. Farther back Smyth's platoon formed a second wedge in front of the softskinned ground vehicles Sergeant Major Ogren commanded.

They soon reached the junction Corporal Ennis had labeled phaseline Orange. As the formation veered west, Bull noted with relief that there was little traffic on the road in front of them, even though it was a sunny workday. On that thought Bull put his binoculars to his face and peered out into the fields. He was reassured to see farmers working their fields, some even waving to the moving convoy, mistaking their action for training maneuvers.

Bull did not expect trouble this close to the Slammers' base. If there was going to be trouble, it would be nearer the wreck. The enemy would be more likely to attack helpless survivors than to tangle with armed soldiers. The town of Plains swept into his view. He gave it a careful search, then inspected the area around it for anything unusual. The forests on his right were Dyer's concern, but the mountain to the west beyond Plains was Bull's worry. He'd have to worry a little longer, because he was still too far away to resolve any worthwhile details.

"Foxtrot, this is Six. Widen it to two hundred," Bull ordered, telling his command to increase the gap between vehicles to two hundred meters. The increase would not reduce their ability to react to a situation but would make it hard for an attacker to switch targets rapidly. Bull breathed a bit easier.

"Approaching Aqua," Dyer reported. "Request permission to recon."

"Negative," Bull replied. They were indeed very close to the town of Plains, designated phaseline Aqua.

"Foxtrot Alpha India, detail a recon to Aqua," Bull told Lieutenant Peyton, knowing that he did not want his tanks near the dangers of a narrow-streeted town. The sight of a skimmer squad zigging in front of his tank informed Bull that Peyton had been eager to recon the town. A quick glance behind him confirmed that Peyton hadn't gone himself. The recon squad behaved well. A team dismounted near the edge of the town and disappeared into its outskirts, backed up by the still-mounted second team.

"Foxtrot, reduce speed," Bull radioed, allowing time for the recon team to examine the town.

"This is Foxtrot Alpha India Eight. Aqua is secure," Sergeant Hunt reported shortly after Bull noted the returning pongoes at the town's edge.

"Foxtrot, proceed to Aqua," Bull acknowledged. Timmons accelerated in response. "Foxtrot Alpha India Eight, rejoin your command."

Bull turned around to see how his command was coping

with the newly increased speed. The softskinneds appeared to have bunched up behind Smyth's platoon. "Foxtrot India, increase your pace," he ordered.

The two tank platoons were pinched closer together as they made for the entrance to Plains, but a good knowledge of the roads in the village allowed them to avoid getting entangled. Bull worried that the softskinned vehicles might not perform so well. "Foxtrot India, post road guards for Sierra Major."

"This is Sierra Major," Ogren's raspy voice replied. "Just post one set; I'll have them relieved as I come to them."

"Foxtrot Six, roger," Bull agreed, giving Smyth permission to follow the sergeant major's suggestion. He turned his attention back to his own platoon and ordered, "Lariat, proceed to phaseline Red." He swung his binoculars to the mountain again. It bothered him, especially as watching it would soon become Dyer's responsibility when the combat group followed the road to the southwest.

"Keep a good eye on that mountain," Bull ordered his platoon.

"Yeah, it looks like a real friendly place," Sam Lewis agreed.

"Six, this is Tango Alpha," Dyer interrupted. "We have a possible"—the roar of powerguns drowned him out—"correction, have engaged and destroyed two enemy tanks in the woods to the direct north of Aqua."

Before Bull could reply, two explosions rocked his tank. As the dust cleared, he could see that one of the two shots had struck it a glancing blow.

"Foxtrot, this is Six. Enemy tanks on the mountain! Engage at will!" To Ennis he said, "Find them yet?" Without waiting for Ennis's reply, he radioed Central. "Central, this is Foxtrot. We have engaged and destroyed two enemy tanks and are now being engaged by a further enemy position, number unknown. Out." As he finished speaking, he added, "Sara, send them a spot report. I'll do my own switching."

"On the way," Engles replied.

"Got 'em!" Ennis yelled. On the combat group net he said, "Four enemy tanks, azimuth three-three-five, elevation twenty. Engage."

Bull put his eye to the main gun sights. He quickly got a target on the crosshairs, but another explosion rocked the tank before he could fire.

The enemy has a total of four tanks. Two others were destroyed. Their Ordnance value is 2 per tank.

Lieutenant Bromley's forces are eight hovertanks and twelve squads of skimmer infantry. The Ordnance value of Bull's hovertanks is 4 each, while that of each skimmer infantry squad is 2.

The enemy exchanges no more than three volleys with Group Foxtrot before they retreat. Both the enemy and the Slammers attack using Chart D.

If the enemy succeeds in destroying Group Foxtrot, turn to section 29.

If the enemy is destroyed or driven off, turn to section 27.

— 25 —

It was a hot, sharp engagement. The skimmers could do little but be targets for the explosive shells of the enemy tanks. Hastily, the three infantry officers ducked their platoons into whatever shelter they could find. In most cases that meant sticking tightly to the hovertanks in front of them.

With his section grounded while Sergeant Lewis was bounding with the other section of Foxtrot Tango, Bull saw in his binoculars that his infantry was making itself felt, as one enemy track commander was pulped by small-arms fire. The rest of the enemy personnel hastily ducked inside the protection of their tanks. Bull's tanks, not having to "button up," had that much better a chance of scoring hits on the enemy.

The roar of his powergun told him that Corporal Ennis needed no urging from him to engage the enemy. The sudden shattering explosion of one of the tanks on the hill told him that his corporal's aim was true.

"Good going, Keith!" Bull roared over the intercom. He swept his binoculars across the hill but could see nothing but smoke.

"Foxtrot, this is Alpha Tango. Enemy destroyed," Dyer reported.

"Two Six, Two Zero," Lewis said on his heels. "Enemy destroyed or withdrawn."

"Very well," Bull replied. "Foxtrot reform. Good shooting."

As always, Bull found himself drained at the end of the encounter. He felt the soreness of tensed muscles and an adrenaline drain as his body adjusted to the fact that he had survived again.

If Bull had had any doubts about how much trouble he would have getting to the wreck, they were dashed now. Ahead of them, across an expanse of blue water, lay Heatherlake, phaseline Green. It was a medium-sized city with a suburb on the near side of the two lakes from which the cities got their name.

Bull wasn't too worried about Little Heatherlake, but the city of Heatherlake itself could hide a whole battalion, which would require more than his small force to dislodge.

"Casualties are pretty light, sir," Engles reported to him.

"Thanks," Bull acknowledged. It was time for the next move. Bull decided that he had three choices: go south through the forests and avoid the city altogether, send his infantry in a stealthy pincer recon around the city, or advance with his infantry backed up by the tanks.

Keep track of the Slammers' casualties on the chart on page xiv. Put a pencil check in the box for each unit that was destroyed in the battle.

If Bull goes south and takes the lower route, turn to section 45.

If Bull continues on his current route, using a skimmer recon formation, turn to section 48.

If Bull continues on his current route and uses the skimmers to assault, turn to section 49.

— 26 —

It was no decision, really.

"This is Foxtrot Six," Bull said over the group push. "Proceed to phaseline Lavender." He glanced at his watch. "Increase speed, tanks forward." The way things were going, he saw no reason to slow down until they reached the mountains.

Outside of Glendale, the hill to his left loomed larger. It was far enough away that he couldn't detail a skimmer squad to check it out, but near enough to worry him. He allowed it to distract him, knowing that Dyer was guarding the more vulnerable flank on the open plains, although Dyer had showed himself to be a bit too eager in his declaration of the securing of Glendale. That's why it took more than a moment for Bull to notice the groundcar approaching his convoy on the road.

His reactions were still swift. "Foxtrot, ground!" He braced himself as Timmons reacted to the order. "Approach that vehicle, Timmons!" Bull ordered. The supertank lurched as Timmons poured power into the fans and lowered the nose of the tank to let it gain the speed he had started to kill.

The groundcar halted before Bull's tank reached it. A figure emerged. Bull restrained himself as he realized it was unarmed.

"Cover me!" Bull ordered, grabbing his sidearm and jumping from the tank. The figure beside the car started toward him. "Forget it," Bull told his crew. The first strides of the figure had told him exactly who it was.

Bull licked his lower lip and tasted the blood that was still fresh where it had been split the night before. He asked himself if this was why he had gone toward the mountains. How quickly events can make one forget, he mused, and then reality brings the past into sharp focus once more. Standing before him, long hair flowing, was the girl he and Peter Smyth had fought over the night before.

"Donna," Bull said to her. "Go back home."

She was startled, and faltered. "You?" She looked behind him. "Peter, too?" Bull nodded. "Then it's just as well I came. I would have come anyway, not knowing who it was."

"What?"

"There are two tanks up ahead, beyond town. They're in the forest east of the road waiting to ambush you," she told him quickly. "I heard about it from a farmer. I knew someone would come. I had to give this warning." She looked up into his eyes. "I'm glad it was you."

"Thank you." He turned to go back to his tank, then turned back again. "Donna—"

She leaned up and kissed him. "There's still a choice to be made," she told him.

Bull frowned, shaking his head. "There is no choice." He caressed her cheek. "There never was a choice." He dropped his hand and turned away. "Thanks for telling me," he said as he left.

Back at the tank, Bull pondered. Donna Mills had no great reason to love him, although at one time she thought she might. Her family lived in Nickel Run, at the foot of the Crags. It was just possible they had been taken captive and used to force her to give him that information. Maybe the enemy hoped to slow him down, to confuse him, or force him to turn away. It was possible.

If Bull disregards Donna's advice, turn to section 33.

If Bull decides to act on Donna Mills's advice, turn to section 31.

— 27 —

A cyan bolt tore from Bull's tank as he kicked the pedal, sundering the turret of an enemy tank. The enemy tank caught fire from the shot and exploded when the blaze reached its ammunition. Beside him the rest of his platoon poured cold, calculated, withering fire that tore the top off the mountain. Bolt after cyan bolt touched the mountain and rendered it to atoms.

It was a short, sharp engagement, much as Bull had expected. As soon as he started traversing the turret in search of another target, he realized that all the targets were either destroyed or had pulled back.

"Cease fire!" He called over the radio. "Report."

"Tango Alpha, no casualties," Lieutenant Dyer replied calmly.

"India Alpha, we're still combat ready," Lieutenant Peyton informed him.

"Lost a couple of men, but we can still fight," the leader of India Bravo reported.

"This is India, ready to move," Pete Smyth replied. Bull grinned. With Smyth it was always "Ready to move." It had been a joke between them, a bitter joke that had started one day several weeks ago when Smyth's strength was down to ten men and Bull had only two tanks. Bull had asked him if he felt they should withdraw to get more men and equipment, and Smyth had replied, "Ready to move."

The hill smoldered, and a dust cloud hung over it in testimony to the might of the powerguns. Any nearby enemy would know that something was happening, that someone was coming.

They were ready to move. Bull considered the roads ahead. They could alter course and head up toward Heatherlake, a large city and an excellent spot to be ambushed by well-protected infantry. Bull decided against that in an instant.

Keep track of the Slammers' casualties on the chart on page xiv.

Put a pencil check in the box for each unit that was destroyed in the battle, and turn to section 45.

— 28 —

"Foxtrot, advance to Lavender, Skimmers forward," Bull ordered, sticking with the planned course of action.

"Lariat Two Six, this is Papa One Six, over," Lieutenant Smyth radioed on Bull's platoon push.

"Go ahead," Bull replied. The only reason Smyth would have to not use the combat group frequency was to talk semiprivately with Bull.

"I'd like to send Alpha India to the far side of that hill in a wide pincer," Smyth told him. "I think we need the extra safety it guarantees."

"No," Bull decided swiftly. "That platoon is too green for a maneuver like that. They'd report every rabbit that hopped out there. We charge on. You keep your eyes open and we'll be all right."

"Roger," Smyth agreed, but his tone said otherwise. "Out."

Bull sighed. Smyth's request was good combat sense in a known combat situation. Time was too important now for Bull to decide automatically that there was a chance of combat, especially in light of current experience. He hoped Smyth wasn't being too edgy.

Smyth

"Foxtrot India, this is Six. Over," Bull called on the group push, knowing that Smyth would have switched back.

"This is India," Smyth replied.

"I want a pincer recon to secure Lavender. You may use all India elements. Tango elements will provide defensive fire on your command," Bull told him. There, he thought to himself, that'll give Pete enough to stiffen his spine.

"India, wilco," Smyth replied, confirming the order.

The combat group had rounded the hill now and the road angled northeast toward Cullea. To their left were open plains except where the road snaked back northwest from Cullea. There, forests masked the beginnings of the great Crags. Behind the trees lay the village of Nickel Run—phaseline Rust—where Donna Mills lived.

Bull wondered if the girl he and Smyth had fought over the night before was still thinking of them, or whether she had forgotten all about them. Bull doubted it. Now there's a girl with a problem, Bull noted. She was also a problem for him. If only he could get her to see reason. Rudely, he forced such thoughts from his mind and returned to the situation at hand.

His hovertanks had reached the spot occupied by the skimmers moments before. The skimmers could be seen occasionally flitting about as they jockeyed to get their positions in the pincer. Bull paid scant attention to Smyth's orders, knowing that whatever else he was, Pete Smyth was certainly able to conduct a simple recon pincer formation.

"Bravo, set," the platoon leader of Foxtrot Bravo India reported.

"Alpha, set," Lieutenant Peyton added. Both pincer platoons were set and in position.

"Proceed," Smyth replied calmly. Bull knew that Pete was sweating with fear that clung to all men who had seen the same combat maneuver fall apart under fire. Their positions might look great, their cover might be excellent, but it was never enough. And now they had to operate without the benefit of satellite surveillance, the same surveillance that had saved their bacon so many times before.

A puff of smoke made Bull start, but it was only a skimmer covering some dusty road. All the same he swore; such a sign would alert anyone to their presence. Seconds stretched their existence out as though alive and clinging to their moments. Bull forced himself to be calm, but he jumped when a voice on the radio said, "This is India. Lavender is secure."

"This is Foxtrot. Set for Rust," Bull replied, forcing himself to swallow before he spoke again. "Tango, this is Foxtrot. Take positions to the far side of Lavender. Sierra Major, proceed to Lavender."

The air seemed alive again, and the throb of the huge hover fans intruded once more on Bull's hearing as the tanks moved toward Cullea. They arrived in short order, and when they got there, it was apparent nothing was out of the ordinary. Bull chided himself for both his earlier unconcern about everything and his hypercaution in the approach to Cullea. I'm getting old, he thought to himself. It was the ancient curse a soldier used.

Turn to section 34.

— 29 —

The ground boiled around them. Bolts of powergun lightning flashed while Timmons struggled to twist the sturdy supertank out of harm's way.

"Retreat! Retreat!" A voice cried over the laserlink. Bull thought it sounded like Bravo India.

Suddenly his world rocked and lurched and he felt himself thrown hard against the turret. Recovering slowly, he called out, "Ennis! What's the situation?"

"Ennis got it," Engles told him. "He got it." Is that how Engles sounds when she's crying? Bull wondered.

Bull looked out and saw that his tank was wedged firmly against the ground. More powergun bolts streaked by: fat, red cyan and thinner blue-green; all too near.

"Lewis! We're wedged! Give me a nudge!" Bull called to his platoon sergeant, vainly trying to search out the other tanks of his platoon in the dust of battle. Around him all he could see was smoke and fire.

"Lewis got it, too," Engles reported. "Try Gleeson." An explosion burst into deadly brilliance beside them. "That was Gleeson," Engles noted dully.

"Out!" Timmons shouted. "We've got to get out!" He started to scramble out of the driver's hatch.

"Stay where you are!" Bull ordered. "We'll get help!" Switching frequencies, he called, "Smyth! My tank's hit, platoon's out of it! I need help."

"We've got to get out!" Timmons screamed, crawling out of his hatch. A bright streak silhouetted his head and shoulders for a brief second, and then he was gone, his body spread all over the front of the turret.

"Ennis! Ennis, get to the driver's seat!" Bull ordered.

"He's dead!" Engles screamed. "I told you already, he's dead!" Bull turned to her, to lash out, to scream, to deny it all. He was stopped in mid-motion by an intense flash of white light. An enemy bolt had struck the turret, melting the hull and vaporizing it instantly. Molten iridium flowed toward him along the floor and splattered him from above. Bull clutched his face in agony, one eye seared through by the molten metal. Another bolt struck his tank, shattering the already ruined turret and twisting it around with the force.

Bull forced his remaining eye to stay open, and saw the softskinned vehicles torn up by bolts of rainbow-hued brilliance.

"Pretty!" Engles said from nearby, her voice hoarse with hysteria. "It's pretty." Then a bolt caught her and shattered her body against the hull, flesh smeared and blood streaming.

Bull was still turning toward her when something hot creased his shoulder. He tried to focus his one eye and began to shudder uncontrollably at the sight of his blackened bones sticking out.

"Oh, you Stars!" he swore, and crumpled to the molten floor of the tank.

"Donna? Donna what have I done? Donna . . . Colonel? Sir, my men—"

The victims at the crash site were massacred with their own weapons. There were scenes of intense bravery: doctors sheltering the wounded with their own bodies, men using just their bodies to try to halt the oncoming enemy, armless wounded flinging themselves back into battle.

But it was all for nothing. No help arrived. The charred hulks of the relief convoy were surrounded by an honor guard of burned-out tanks and smoldering skimmers.

"I promised you, Hammer!" Gesparde Jebbitt swore, surveying his proud men. "Now you will die!"

You have failed. If you wish to try again to attempt the rescue of the Slammers Down!, please turn to section 1.

— 30 —

They left the town and headed west to the crossroads. The fighting and the wreckage ahead were only kilometers away and plainly visible. Many of his officers grumbled when Bull made them turn and follow the road north toward the wreck nearest the road. Pete Smyth was mute, but his skimmers were fleet and made good time.

To their left, scant one kilometer from them, was the first fall of the wreck. The transport had been huge, carrying almost a full third of the Slammers. Companies of infantry, armor, and combat cars had been aboard, to say nothing of batteries of the regimental artillery. Colonel Hammer had learned early to move his force in discrete, battle-ready units. This was the only time it had worked against him, providing his enemy with all the components of a full fighting force.

The wreck was facing away from them, scattered toward the mountain beyond. Ahead, Bull thought he could make out parts of the great propulsion units and cargo doors, but he couldn't be sure; there was so much twisted wreckage and splintered debris.

"Request permission to secure Iridium," Pete Smyth radioed.

The request took Bull aback. Smyth had earned it, fighting well enough, but Bull was in command. Still, there might be good reasons to have the skimmers be the first to contact his battle-wearied comrades.

If Bull lets the skimmers secure phaseline Iridium, turn to section 21.

If Bull decides to secure phaseline Iridium with his tanks, turn to section 134.

— 31 —

And snowball fights in Hell were also possible. Probably more likely, too. Bull shook his head to dislodge any uncharitable thoughts he might have about Donna Mills. If she had been coerced, she would have found a way to let him know. The warning was true, the danger real.

Bull said to his unit, "Foxtrot, just had a pleasant birdy tell us about two bears in the woods beyond Lavender. We'll be spotted by them as soon as we round this mountain. I want all eyes peeled. They're expecting to find us surprised; let's surprise them.

"All you little friendlies make sure you're behind the big boys," Bull added, meaning that the skimmers should close in behind his tanks. "I don't see any reason for you to get the bitter end of this match. You may support as soon as we have engaged. Out."

To his own platoon Bull said, "Lariat Two, this is Six. Make sure you hit those fools. If the little guys don't know how to tag along, don't worry."

"You'll need another case of beer!" Sergeant Gleeson called back. Bull smiled. It was his custom to give a case of beer to the tank crew that destroyed an enemy tank on the first shot. Gleeson's Eightball tank crew had decorated the left side of their turret with beer case symbols, one per hit, to display their prowess.

"Foxtrot, this is Six. Advance," Bull told his combat group. "Central, Sara," he requested from his comm. chief.

"There already," Sara Engles informed him in a bored tone.

"Central, this is Foxtrot. We are about to engage two tanks. Over," Bull radioed.

"Roger." Bull recognized the voice of Major Pritchard. "Spot report when you've completed the action."

"Ennis, *I* want a case this time," Bull said to his corporal.

"I could use a cold one, too, sir," Corporal Ennis replied. "I still haven't found them. Switching to IR." Ennis thumbed the switch on his helmet that brought down the infrared display. With his binoculars Bull scanned the forest. He guessed where the enemy would set themselves up and swiveled the turret. "Got 'em!" Ennis yelled. "Fire!"

With a quick glance at the sights, Bull kicked the pedal for the huge powergun. The massive hovertank lurched slightly with the recoil of the powergun, and a bright beam of death lanced across the fields.

The enemy has a total of two tanks, both concealed in the forest. Their Ordnance value is 2 each.

Bull Bromley's forces are eight hovertanks and twelve squads of skimmers, including Lieutenant Smyth's platoon. Bull's panzers have an Ordnance value of 4 each, while his skimmer infantry has an Ordnance value of 2 per squad.

The enemy exchanges no more than three volleys with Combat Group Foxtrot before retreating. The enemy uses Chart D; the Slammers use Chart B.

If the enemy succeeds in destroying Group Foxtrot, turn to section 29.

If the enemy is destroyed or driven off, turn to section 53.

— 32 —

It was a nightmare conceived of light: blue-green, hideous cyan, and the furious white of exploding vehicles. Here and there Bull could see that some of his own men had had enough, crouching beside their torn skimmers and only barely returning fire. Bull's platoon, under his orders, saved the day by decimating the infantry at phaseline Gold and then occupying the rubble, securing the way for the rest of his command and deftly assaulting the remaining enemy tanks. Either the enemy had decided they'd had enough or they ran out of ammunition, because the fighting stopped shortly afterward. Looking back, Bull could see the plains were littered with smoldering vehicles of all descriptions, including some of the precious softskinneds.

Finally it was over. The roaring stopped and the screaming

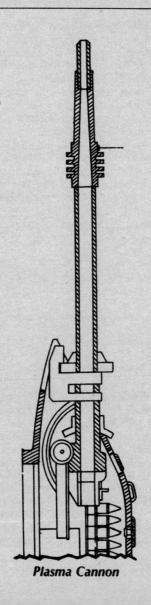

Plasma Cannon

started. "November Fower Mike, Victor will take your wounded. Move out!" Bull ordered harshly as the smoke from the wreck rose visibly just down the road.

One by one the tanks of Group Foxtrot roared through the remnants of Regarra and on to Iridium.

Turn to section 30.

— 33 —

He couldn't believe her. Her knowledge of military matters was too limited. Even if she had seen something in the forest, it was probably a farm truck or a tractor. The evidence was too slim to force him to change his mind.

"Foxtrot, proceed to Lavender, all haste," Bull ordered. He had wasted enough time.

"All haste, sir?" Timmons inquired eagerly.

"That's right," Bull replied, and wished he hadn't when the surge of power Timmons forced from the tank's fusion reactor slammed him against the hatch.

The tanks roared up to the town of Cullea and straight through it. Inside the town the tanks swerved and scraped their rusty skirts against the ground as Timmons's blistering pace forced them to take tight turns. From Bull's turret the town was a mere blur of startled faces and a few dull shop windows. Even so, he and Ennis, both exposed in their hatches, were apprehensive and gripped their weapons protectively. A tightness in Bull loosened as they left the town. Wide open spaces were safer.

"Foxtrot, this is Sierra Major. We can't keep up," the sergeant major reported.

"This is Foxtrot. We'll have to slow down somewhere between Rust and Blue," Bull reported. "You can catch up then." Devil take it all, with the wind in his hair and the country whipping by him, Bull didn't think for a moment that anything could stop him and his panzers. They were fast approaching the forest in front of Nickel Run. At this rate we'll get to the survivors in plenty of time, Bull thought cheerfully.

Turn to section 34.

— 34 —

A cyan flash from the forest just in front of them coupled with a dull explosion near his tank caused Bull to realize that he had made a big mistake. Two more shells rapidly followed the first.

"Return fire!" Bull yelled over his mike. "Pulverize that forest!" As his tank lurched with the recoil of the huge powergun, Bull cursed his rashness and hoped the price for it wouldn't be too high.

Two enemy tanks have surprised Bull and his command. The Slammers are out in the open; the enemy is hidden in the forest. The enemy tanks have an ordnance value of 2 each. They exchange only three volleys with Bull's combat group before withdrawing.

Bull's command consists of eight hovertanks with an Ordnance value of 4 each and twelve squads of skimmer infantry with an Ordnance value of 2 per squad.

The enemy fire using Chart B; the Slammers fire using Chart D.

If Bull's command is destroyed, turn to section 29.

If the enemy withdraws or is destroyed, turn to section 53.

— 35 —

"Request permission to occupy Gold," Smyth relayed. His platoon had made it to the outskirts of the village.

"Roger." Ahead, Bull watched as the well-trained platoon probed, pincered, and occupied the smoldering town.

"Gold secure," Bull heard. They were almost there. He could clearly see the smoke of the transport wreck and, through his binoculars, some of the larger sections that had broken off in the crash.

Turn to section 30.

— 36 —

The earth shook and the sky was a blaze of deadly bolts going to and from the enemy. Skimmers were blazed into oblivion and tanks rocked and rolled with near hits or death blows. The Slammers reeled under a well-prepared assault, well executed. The enemy had forgotten nothing.

Nothing except the men they were fighting. Battered, bloodied, torn to shreds, the individual Slammers responded to the rain of death with one of their own. Like a flaming phoenix, the Slammers poured back thick and thin cyan powerbolts to the doom of the enemy.

Suddenly there was no more fire. The enemy had had enough. They had withdrawn or were dead, Bull didn't care. Plumes of dust blown up by powerbolts lifted across the battlefield and mixed with burnt metal and shredded flesh. The air reeked of torn atoms, torn metal, and torn men. Now, before the shock could get to them, Bull had to move his men on.

"November Fower Mike, continue the operations. Leave the wounded for the softskinneds," Bull ordered calmly.

And just as calmly, Smyth replied, "Roger."

Turn to section 35.

— 37 —

Bravo India was decimated. Bull, hardened to battle and veteran of many, could hardly believe his eyes. Skimmer after skimmer flared and vanished as cyan powerbolts caught and vaporized them. A few received only glancing blows, flying through the air fifty or sixty meters before coming to rest as bent blood-covered metal. Peyton's platoon received slightly better treatment, having the cover of the terrain to protect it. Smyth's platoon, identified at the first firing, was in the open, but grounded soon and gave as good as it got.

Group Foxtrot's tanks gave better than they got, but Bull would have to write letters to loved ones all the same. Foxtrot had been battered before, now it was bowing.

"Move out!" Bull ordered. "We'll get the casualties on the way!"

"But—"

"Move out!" Bull roared.

"On the way," Smyth replied in weary tones. Far ahead, Bull could see dust as India platoon moved out. To the left Peyton's platoon headed for the next forest west, around the little hill on the near side, while on the right the remnants of Bravo India reformed under Dyer's lead and occupied the forest so recently abandoned by their assailers.

"Mike, this is November Niner Zero. I can see firing ahead," Dyer relayed quietly in a voice that spoke of respect, admiration, and sorrow.

"Best speed," Bull replied. They were almost there.

"Mike Two Zero, Juliet Niner Zero. Enemy infantry occupying phaseline Gold," Smyth reported.

"Via!" Bull swore. Then, collecting himself, he ordered, "Target it for me. I'll barrage it along with the rest of the tanks while you assault."

"Just take the whole town," Smyth replied. "I wouldn't want you to miss anything."

"Roger." To Gleeson, Bull said, "Keep a few rounds in reserve, but no more!"

Together the two tanks began a slow, steady, utterly destructive barrage on the unsuspecting town from a distance of over twenty kilometers. Vainly the enemy tried to respond with buzzbombs, but most grounded well before they made the distance, and only left better targets for Dyer's and Lewis's sections as Bull committed the rest of his tanks. It was a slaughter.

The enemy has a platoon of skimmer-mounted infantry in the town: four squads, each with an Ordnance value of 2. The enemy attacks using Chart F and withdraws after three rounds of combat.

The Slammers attack using Chart B.

If the Slammers are destroyed, turn to section 29.

If the enemy withdraws or is defeated, turn to section 35.

— **38** —

"Mike Two Zero, Juliet Niner Zero," Smyth called softly. "Two Zero."

"Spot report: four enemy tanks in the woods just west of—" Smyth broke off and reappeared on a lower channel. "Alpha Niner Zero, ground!"

"Roger," Peyton replied calmly. "Spot report."

"I think we've got it already," Bromley replied. "November Niner Zero, we have contact on the right."

"November Niner Zero, contact on the left. Enemy tanks in the woods to the northwest."

"Suggestions?" Bull asked. The situation was not good. His command was not in shape to tackle two enemy tank platoons, especially platoons equipped with hovertanks.

"Charge!" Bravo India's leader roared. Startled, Bull turned to see that Bravo India was indeed charging straight for the enemy. "You copping dats had better get them on the first shot!" their leader yelled to Bull.

"Mike, this is Two Zero. Engage on flashes only!" Bull roared. It was too late to stop brave but reckless Bravo India. All Bull could do was hope to profit by their mad charge.

The enemy has two hovertank platoons of four hovertanks each, with an Ordnance value of 4 per tank. They are not too startled to wield crippling blows to Bravo India. They attack using Chart D. The enemy runs out of ammunition and flees after three rounds of combat.

The Slammers attack using Chart B. They have the advantage of being able to sight on the stationary enemy with their unseen hovertanks. All Slammer losses must come first from Bravo India, then from other Slammer units.

If the Slammers are destroyed, turn to section 29. If the Slammers survive the attack, turn to section 37.

— 39 —

The Skimmers saved the day. Bull swore red and blue with rage, but it was the skimmers that saved the day. They charged in among the combat cars and forced them to maintain straight lines for Bull's tanks to hit. Many men lost their lives as they played "chicken" with the combat cars, but more dealt death blows to their drivers and lived to tell the tale. Bravo India's leader, in a daring stroke, took out the entire crew of a car and used its guns to destroy yet another.

Their casualties were high, but the Slammers had won. The enemy was either dead or crippled and had withdrawn. But they still had to get to the wreck.

"November Fower Mike, this is Mike Two Zero. Proceed to Gold." With a word to Timmons, Bull's tank set off at full speed to set the example.

They made good time and were on the approach to Regarra in ten minutes. Bull's tanks came very close to the town before he decided that he wouldn't risk them once more.

"Put a round on it," he told Ennis.

Dutifully, the young corporal laid a bright cyan round on the approach road to town. Instantly the flare of a buzzbomb replied.

"Let's show them who we are!" Bull roared. In unison the great guns of the hovertanks roared back.

The enemy has one platoon of four squads of skimmer-mounted infantry in the town. They each have an Ordnance value of 2 and attack using Chart D. The enemy withdraws after three rounds.

The Slammers attack using Chart B.

If the Slammers are destroyed, turn to section 29.

If the Slammers survive, turn to section 52.

— 40 —

Smyth's platoon took no chances with the town of Regarra, phaseline Gold. They cautiously lobbed a few rounds of light fire into the town, and when the enemy opened up, Smyth called on his tank section to level the city.

The enemy has one platoon of four squads of skimmer-mounted infantry. Each squad has an Ordnance value of 2. The enemy fights using Chart E, and withdraws after three rounds.

The Slammers, using mostly their long-range tanks, fight using Chart B.

If the enemy destroys the Slammers, turn to section 29.

If the enemy withdraws or is defeated, turn to section 44.

— 41 —

The enemy fought well, charging out of their hiding places to duel it out with the hovertanks. But the great guns outmatched the tribarrels, while the little skimmers played a dangerous, deadly game of cat and mouse with the lethal cars. Some of the skimmers lost the battle, particularly those of Bravo India.

Bull could not figure out how so many of Bravo India's untested trainees survived. He watched in stunned amazement as its platoon leader stormed up the side of a car to kill its crew and use its gun to set fire to another enemy combat car.

Then firing stopped. The air cleared of smoke but still reeked of burnt flesh and soon filled with the cries of the wounded.

"Victor, help the wounded," Bull pleaded. He looked through his binoculars, trying to assess his scattered command.

It was not as strong as it had been, nor as lively. It could still fight—it had to. "Move out!" he told them. "Leave the wounded by the road for Victor."

Ahead, Smyth's platoon crossed the road and left a few men. Peyton's platoon left more men, while Bravo's left none. Bravo had only living and dead—no wounded.

Turn to section 40.

Barrage after barrage from the fast tribarrels roared into Bull's command. Their reply was just as hot, however, and proved to be the enemy's undoing. In short order flaming wrecks on both sides burned and the enemy fled, either out of ammunition or, more likely, out of nerve.

But the results were similar on Bull's side. His Slammers were now dangerously low on ammunition and men. Bravo India had been poorly positioned from the start and, after receiving scathing fire throughout the battle, was now only a shadow of its original strength. But Bull wouldn't swap those remnants for anything. Bravo's leader had single-handedly stormed a combat car and shot the crew at point-blank range. Then he'd fired on another enemy car with the first car's gun.

Peyton's platoon had fought skillfully and steadily. Smyth accounted for himself excellently, dispatching the first platoon he went against and then aiding Peyton to finish off the other platoon. The field was theirs. So were most of the wounded.

"Victor, get the wounded," Bull snapped, too frazzled to be polite. "Move out," he told his command. "We have to get to that wreck soon."

"Full speed!" Sergeant Major Ogren agreed. Ahead of Bull the wounded collected by the road, dropped off by their comrades. The Skimmers and hovertanks charged forward to reach the northern straight in five minutes.

Turn to section 40.

— 43 —

They made good time. Peyton's skimmers were stuck in the first forest, worrying about something odd, but Bull's tanks and the softskinneds were almost past them. On infrared Bull could make out several bright spots, but he wasn't convinced they were anything other than rocks that had basked in the sun. Smyth's command had charged on obliviously, although he had sent a detachment into the northern forest on the right, while Dyer was just reaching his area.

A rapid barrage of light on his left side caught Bull unawares, and it was a moment before he could see again. Then he caught the movement of large, fast objects as they tore out of the forest and headed for the softskinneds, guns blazing. Combat cars!

"Via, they've copping well got cars!" someone swore.

"Stop them!" Bull roared, swinging his barrel to put action to words. Suddenly a second barrage erupted and he could see that Dyer's group had stumbled on to another nest of combat cars.

"We're being attacked!" Smyth called from ahead. "Request assistance."

"Negative!" Bull roared back.

The enemy has three platoons of combat cars, four cars in each platoon. Each car has an Ordnance value of 3. They have surprised the Slammers and attack using Chart B. The enemy withdraws after three rounds because of a shortage of ammunition.

The Slammers attack using Chart C.

If the Slammers are destroyed, turn to section 29.

If the enemy withdraws or is destroyed, turn to section 42.

— 44 —

You could hardly call it a battle. A battle is a two-sided thing. Bull's tanks poured flaming round after cyan round into the town until nothing was left standing and nothing could move. Then Smyth's platoon cautiously went forward and secured the smoldering wreck that was Regarra. Bull felt much sympathy for the townspeople and hoped they had escaped when the enemy arrived, but he and his men had no time to waste.

"November Fower Mike, proceed to Iridium," Bull ordered. The cheers that came back to him more than made up for the flames of Regarra.

Turn to section 30.

— 45 —

That left him only the decision of what formation and tactics to use. They would be entering the forest, perfect infantry terrain. It was obvious that his infantry would go first. The question was whether they should go on recon far ahead of his tanks and pincer to either side of the road, or whether they should go with the tanks just behind them, ready to lend support.

Between Smithtown, phaseline Red and Tooey, phaseline Amber, Bull would hardly be able to reorganize his command, so the right decision was critical. He thought about it carefully.

If Bull chooses the infantry recon, turn to section 46.

If Bull chooses to position the tanks just behind the infantry, turn to section 47.

— 46 —

It was difficult terrain. The road itself was surrounded by clumps of forest, but to either side was wide open spaces. The forest could hold an ambush fronted with buzzbombs which would spell disaster for his tanks. He couldn't afford to simply burn the forests away. He didn't have the ammunition, he didn't have the time, and he couldn't afford the repercussions with the Maffrens.

If he sent his infantry in far-flung formations, his tanks would be little able to support them. On the flip side, his infantry would be able to spot any ambush centered on the road. That was his mission: to clear that road.

"Foxtrot India, this is Foxtrot, come down and talk," Bull said. It was an old agreed-upon signal between him and Pete Smyth to switch to their special frequency. "Sara, we're—"

"—going down, sir," she finished for him.

"Pete?"

"Here," Smyth replied.

"I'm going to ask you: will you lead? We've had our arguments, but I need a strong leader. Will you lead? 'Cause I'm going to send the skimmers out first," Bull said carefully. There was a long silence.

"That's what I'd do," Smyth agreed. "You going to back me up, Mr. First Lootenan'?" Smyth joked.

"Only if you call hopping at your every request backing you up," Bull returned.

"I'll need just that," Smyth said. "Brad, this is the kind of terrain that's just evil."

"I know," Bull agreed. The terrain could hold snipers, tanks, mines, skimmers, anything. And the worst of it was, the terrain would still look innocent. "Can we handle it?"

Smyth snorted. "Can it handle us?"

That's what I wanted to hear! Bull thought to himself.

Aloud he said, "You've got the reins. Let's go." Bull switched frequencies without waiting for Smyth to acknowledge.

"Foxtrot, this is Six," Bull said when he was back on the regular channel. "We're regrouping. India will command Indias Bravo and Alpha. Tango and Alpha Tango will support. This is in effect until we reach phaseline Amber."

"Indias Bravo and Alpha, this is Foxtrot India," Smyth came on just then. "We will travel in platoon wedge formation until further orders. Alpha will take the left flank, Bravo the right. Tango and Alpha Tango will provide support to the left and right flanks. Prepare to move out."

"This is Tango, roger," Bull acknowledged. Ennis gave him a wondering look as Timmons slowed down their tank to allow the skimmers past. "Relax, Keith. We'll be in front when it counts," Bull told him.

"Move out," Smyth said in a controlled voice. Bull nodded to himself. He felt that way, too, when he was in command. It was a strange feeling, knowing that over a hundred people obeyed your orders—and could die for your mistakes.

They covered the remaining kilometers to phaseline Red, Smithtown, in short order. Smyth charged right into the town with bravado, although Bull had watched him use his binoculars all the way up to the gates of the town. They moved through and around the town and made the turn in the road that started northwest again.

The hill where the enemy had fired upon them still lay on their right, but the sun was coming from their back. Twenty short kilometers ahead lay the first of the forests. Smyth made a sharp decision and sent his two flanking platoons far out to either side of the road, kilometers out in an enveloping maneuver around that first forest.

With his two platoons so far-flung, Smyth asked the two tank platoons to close in somewhat. They continued this way until they were nearly three kilometers from the forest. By this time Alpha had arrived at the northwest corner of the forest and Bravo had occupied the next forest north of the one surrounding the road.

Bravo's platoon leader called up nervously, "We think we spotted something, sir!"

"What is it?" Smyth asked testily.

"I'm not sure; would you take a look?" the platoon leader asked timidly.

"Put it on our screens," Smyth replied, and switched the image over so Bull could also see it.

It was hard to tell what was out there. One moment Smyth thought he saw tanks, but the next moment the forest appeared quiet.

If Bull changes his plans because of what he sees, turn to section 60.

If Bull continues in the current formation, turn to section 61.

— 47 —

The terrain ahead would be difficult. It was the sort of terrain that worried tankers and pongoes alike. Bull frowned. If he sent the skimmers far ahead by themselves, they'd be dogmeat if they met up with any serious opposition. If he sent his hovertanks out first, they'd be eaten by hidden buzzbombs before his infantry would have a chance of finding them. He decided he would send the skimmers up front with the tanks tight in behind. Each could support the other; that was the theory of combined arms that had worked so well for centuries.

"Foxtrot, this is Six. We will reform. Skimmers in front, tanks tight in behind. India, you will have the van. India Alpha, you get the right flank. India Bravo, you take the left. Tango Alpha, the left also. Tango will take the right." He paused. "We'll hold this formation until phaseline Amber—there's no room to alter it until then."

The five platoons formed into the new formation rapidly, but not so rapidly that the trailing softskinned vehicles couldn't catch up. Their advance to phaseline Red, Smithtown, was rapid and uneventful. Smyth's platoon charged through the town without a pause; he had reconnoitered thoroughly with his binoculars. Besides, the tanks they had driven off from the hill had held command of the town. It was far too unlikely that anyone would place a force in the town also.

As they moved through Smithtown, they turned sharply to the right, onto a road leading northwest, in almost a straight line with their goal. Beyond Smithtown they crossed vast plains until they finally met up with their first worry: a forest that straddled the road. Here Bull worked his unit carefully, sending the infantry forward in leaps and bounds to wait for his huge tanks, which were forced to swerve carefully through the trees or risk toppling one with a telltale crash that the whole forest would recognize.

The huge hovertanks have a Stealth value of 4. Roll two six-sided dice.

If the total of the dice is less than or equal to the tanks' Stealth value, turn to section 62.

If the total is higher than their Stealth value, turn to section 63.

— 48 —

"Show me the map again, Keith," Bull said to Corporal Ennis. Ennis swiveled the display so that the lieutenant could examine it. "Magnify on Heartherlake." The terrain was terrible. Directly to the north was a forest bordered on its west side by a wide lake. Further west of this lake, the road crossed through Little Heatherlake into the town of Heatherlake proper. Beyond the bridge the lake widened once more. It would have to be skimmer recon—but with a difference. Bull peered intently at the map, plotting the routes in his mind. He would send Smyth through the triangular forest to the east of Heatherlake. Dyer would swing around the forest to come into the open at its—Yes!

"Foxtrot this is Six," Bull said over the radio, switching from thought to words. "India will proceed north through the forest to the east of phaseline Green. Alpha Tango will proceed northeast around the forest and charge toward Green when they have rounded the forest. India will support Alpha Tango and suppress fire.

"Foxtrot Tango will follow the road to Green. On my signal, the other two India elements will cross the lake to the east of phaseline Green and secure, rendering aid to Foxtrot Tango on request.

"This divides into two actions: India will command the eastward action, Tango will command the westward action." Bull paused, waiting for any questions. "Execute now."

"Foxtrot India, on the move," Pete Smyth replied. Bull wondered if Smyth was as worried as himself.

"Alpha Tango, moving," Dyer said in reply to some unheard command from Smyth.

"India, inform me when set," Bull told Smyth, meaning that Smyth was to let him know when he had reached the far side of the forest. "Bravo India, you will enter the lake through the forest. Alpha India, follow behind Tango until you can proceed across the lake due north."

"Alpha India, roger." "Bravo, roger," the two infantry leaders acknowledged.

Bull spent the time before Smyth got into position examining the city. Try as he might, he couldn't spot any sign of the enemy. He also couldn't spot much of the normal midday activity he expected to see in a city of fifty thousand people. Infrared was no use; any enemy would have had enough time to camouflage against infrared as well as normal vision. Bull's tanks, with their hot fusion reactors and cooling main guns, would have no such chance.

"Foxtrot Six, India and Alpha Tango set," Smyth informed him calmly.

"Roger," Bull acknowledged. On his platoon frequency he said, "Lariat Two, prepare to advance."

"Two eight." "Two Zero." "Two four," his three subordinates replied quickly, professionally.

"We will enter the lake on the west side of the bridge. Cross with all speed," Bull told them. To his full command he said, "Foxtrot this is Six. Tango is advancing. Move out!" he ordered his platoon. "Gun it, Greg!"

The huge tank lurched as power from the fusion reactor washed through the huge fans. From a standstill the hovertank leaped forward, charging down the side of the road. Air roared by Bull while behind him the ground boiled with dust raised by the fans. Rock steady, the turret remained forward.

"Guns north!" Bull ordered his platoon, swinging his turret towards the city.

The four panzers roared alongside the road and quickly

followed it as it turned northward. They crossed the road to the west and suddenly they were ready.

"Foxtrot, move out!" Bull roared. "Bravo India, Alpha India, move out!"

Suddenly his right flank had sprouted skimmers which appeared as if from nowhere and flitted across the lake. His own tanks slipped onto the lake and started to cross. Bull felt relieved. There appeared to be no enemies in the town.

The harsh report of a powergun blazing to the east of him augmented by several others and the sharper, higher pitched sound of small-arms fire gave him the lie. Further proof, in the form of a buzzbomb skitting across the waters of the lake toward him, was unnecessary.

"Dodge that sucker!" Ennis cried to Timmons.

"Indias Bravo and Alpha, neutralize those buzzards!" Bull cried over the radio, meaning the buzzbomb teams firing at his tanks. They were in a tight situation, and the enemy knew it. Invincible on land, capable of crossing almost any terrain with ease, water was a potential death trap for the huge hovertanks. Crossing water, they had to displace a mass of water to equal their own. To do this the fusion power packs were revved up and the pitch of the hover fans altered, raising the tanks two meters higher. When hovertanks crossed water, they crossed it as high, visible targets. "Hovering ducks!" one Slammer had described them.

Farther away, Bull heard the powerguns of Tango Alpha as Dyer's platoon stormed toward the town. A sudden crescendo of higher-pitched small-arms fire told him that Pete Smyth had engaged the same enemy at closer range.

His tanks had to make it across the lake. Once across, they could be invaluable to his infantry, which even now had gained access to the city and was starting the grim job of slugging it out with an entrenched enemy.

The enemy has two platoons (eight squads) of infantry. Each enemy squad has an Ordnance value of 1. From their entrenched position they fight using Chart C. The enemy exchanges three volleys, then withdraws.

Lieutenant Bromley's Combat Group Foxtrot fights using Chart C as well. Check your Manpower chart to find out how many Slammer units of each type are still available to fight.

If Group Foxtrot is destroyed, turn to section 29.

If the enemy is defeated or driven off, turn to section 55.

— 49 —

Bull swiveled the map display for a closer look. The approaches to Heatherlake were by forest, road, lake, or city. None of them were good tank terrain. Going into Little Heatherlake was probably the worst move. The alternatives were to force the lake at either side of the road or charge into one tip of Heatherlake through the forest. Bull decided to do both.

"Foxtrot India, you will lead all India elements to secure phaseline Green. Suggest that Bravo takes the forest while you and Alpha take the lake. Tango elements will provide support," Bull ordered.

If you have not written "Smyth," turn to section 56.

If you have "Smyth" written down, turn to section 57.

— 50 —

Smyth's platoon saw the enemy before Peyton got to them.
"Mike Two Zero, Juliet Niner Zero. Four Charlie Charlies in the woods to the left," Smyth said calmly, and then, "Via! Four more in the woods on the right!"
"Roger," Bull replied. "Juliet Niner Zero, November Niner Zero, smoke them out."
"Roger," the two commanders replied in unison.
To the left and the right the little skimmers bopped in and out of view of Bull's binoculars, leaping and bounding toward the two woods where the enemy lay. Bull switched his binoculars to infrared but could see no more than before. Switching back, he paused to admire the grace some

of the skimmers showed as they ducked in and out of view.

"To heck with this!" Bravo India's leader called. "Charge!" To Bull's astonishment, the platoon obeyed its wild commander and rushed forward into the open to the waiting tribarrels. The decimation was horrendous.

"Fire!" Bull roared, as the enemy platoon's cyan bolts exposed the combat cars. Dyer's and Bull's two sections fired in unison. Just ahead Smyth yelled, "Another platoon! By the Maker, they've got a third platoon!"

The enemy has three platoons of combat cars, each with four cars. Each car has an Ordnance value of 3. Bravo India's mad charge has given away almost all enemy positions and left the enemy stationary. The enemy attacks using Chart D and withdraws after running out of ammunition three round later.

The Slammers attack using Chart B. All losses are first taken from Bravo India. Any additional losses are applied at the player's discretion.

If the Slammers are destroyed, turn to section 29.

If the enemy withdraws or is destroyed, turn to section 41.

— 51 —

"Mike, this is Two Zero," Bull called. "Juliet elements will be matched with Yankee sections and advance in far pincer recon. All critical terrain will be examined and cleared. November Niner Zero will group with and command Charlie Niner Zero. November One Two will group with Bravo Niner Zero, Bravo Niner Zero commands. Golf One Two will group with Alpha Niner Zero, Alpha Niner Zero commands. Alpha to the left, Bravo in the center, and Charlie on the right."

"Roger," Smyth replied.

"Wilco," Dyer replied.

"Understood," Peyton replied.

"Message received," the obviously disgruntled commander of Bravo India acknowledged.

"Move out."

Three large sections of forest dominated the terrain ahead. Behind the western one were more trees and another danger spot. The terrain was terribly open, good terrain for tanks to attack with overwhelming strength, terrible terrain to clear for a convoy.

Bull's tanks, forming the van for the softskinneds, had to follow the road, first northwest to a junction, then looping back northeast and straightening due north to phaseline Gold. The others were luckier. Peyton's command took off straight for the first forest, leaving smaller patrols to check out the terrain in the immediate vicinity of the road. Dyer's crew headed almost due north into the forest on the right, with Smyth's infantry checking the open space along the whole front.

If you have "Smyth" written down on a piece of paper, turn to section 50.

Otherwise turn to section 43.

— 52 —

The panzers played no games with the enemy infantry. With methodical ease they leveled the town, working from the outside in, trapping the infantry in the rubble and finally in the flame of cyan energy bolts. There was no contest. A stray shot here and there got a few of the skimmers, but the damage was minimal compared with the need for speed. In short order Bull roared, "Move out!"

In silence the Slammers roared through the rubble that had been Regarra.

Turn to section 30.

— 53 —

His first shot was a hit. The turret of the enemy's tank glowed a brilliant white and then the metal flowed, covering its crew and its ammunition. In a second the ammunition exploded. After that he couldn't see anything because of the amount of fire being poured into the forest. Cyan energy streaked into the forest like lightning bolts. Trees arched up into the air, torn by bolts of thunder as the woods were shattered into shell bursts turbid with dirt, tree, and armor. The enemy was destroyed or had fled in terror.

"Cease fire!" Bull called to his troops. "Report."

"India, ready to move," Smyth replied. It was an old joke. During their last campaign, Smyth's platoon had been reduced to ten men and Bull's had been whittled down to two tanks. When Bull had asked if Smyth thought that they should return to base, Smyth replied, "Ready to move." They'd caught Jebbitt's Raiders right after that.

"India Alpha, ready to move," Lieutenant Peyton added in the same tone.

"Foxtrot Alpha, ready to move," Dyer replied stolidly.

"India Bravo, ready to move," the young platoon leader added.

"Sierra Major, on the way," the sergeant major replied.

"Roger," Bull acknowledged. "How'd we do, Sara?" Bull asked his comm. chief, inquiring about his platoon.

"No gripes, Lieutenant," she told him.

Keep track of Slammers' casualties on the chart on page xiv. Put a pencil check in the box for each unit that was destroyed in the battle.

The next phaseline was Rust, the village of Nickel Run and the start of the Crags. After this engagement, Bull was under no delusions about the strength and tenacity of the enemy. They were up against the diehard remnants of Jebbitt's Raiders, men who would stop at nothing to see him dead. He had to outfight them. The Raiders were desperate men, and they would neither give quarter, or show mercy.

"No quarter," Bull said aloud.

"Roger," the sergeant major agreed. "They won't give it, neither will we."

"India, I want a far-flung recon," Bull told Smyth. "I want two elements on either side of the road and the third element to circle behind the mountain and recon there."

"Roger," Smyth acknowledged. "I would like to send India on the far recon."

Bull considered. The terrain was such that the third platoon would be moving about twelve kilometers without any protection, and most likely without communications. The other two platoons would be in sight and communication with Bull's tanks.

"Fair enough," Bull agreed. "Bravo India, you will recon east of the road through the pass. Alpha India will recon west of the road."

"I should like to send my platoon out ten minutes before the others. That'll give us time to get in position and report back," Smyth suggested.

"Move out now. Alpha India, Bravo India, move in ten mikes," Bull agreed.

Smyth's platoon of skimmers silently disappeared eastward. Bull took his binoculars out and tried to track them, but they were so good that he lost sight of them in under a minute, even on infrared. Now all he could do was wait. This maneuver was going to take time, but he was convinced that the enemy might guard this pass—it was too good an opportunity to miss. Slowly the time ticked by.

"Alpha India, Bravo India, move out!" Bull ordered. Over seventy skimmers suddenly shimmered into view and disappeared again as the two platoons moved out to their assigned positions.

"Tango Alpha, be prepared." Bull ordered.

Roll two six-sided dice. If the total is less than or equal to a skimmer squad's Stealth rating (8), turn to section 71.

If the total is greater than the skimmers' Stealth rating, turn to section 72.

— 54 —

"The tanks will go first, followed tight by the infantry, which will cover for the softskinneds," Bull decided. "November gets the right, Golf the left. Alpha, Bravo, and Charlie will follow left to right. Move out!"

The two tank platoons roared out of the town and west toward the road junction. They kept a dispersion of no greater than two hundred meters. Four hundred meters behind them the skimmers followed with a tighter dispersion of fifty meters. Immediately behind the skimmers came the softskinned vehicles carrying the all-important food, medicine, and, most important, ammunition.

They made good time, roaring toward their destination with a speed born of desperation. They reached the junction in five minutes, turned north and were on the curve eastward when Bull spotted something in the forest to the left. It was just a glint at first, but it didn't stay in one place. Bull quickly switched to infrared and was rewarded with the sight of a moving vehicle.

"Golf, prepare to engage to the left," Bull ordered his platoon.

"Combat cars!" Dyer shouted. "There's a platoon of combat cars!" Bull swung and caught sight of the platoon as it roared toward their right flank, jinking left and right to throw off Dyer's aim. On Bull's side it was the same, four gleaming combat cars bright with Slammer colors charged at him. A shocked glance to the front told him that still another platoon was charging from that corner.

"Skimmers, engage!" Bull ordered. The three skimmer platoons gamely charged out toward the enemy while Bull's tanks roared cyan death at the dodging vehicles. A computer kept his sights on his target, but neither it nor he could outguess the car's human driver as he swerved or stopped in front of Bull's powerbolt, pitting his reactions against Brad's. Other cars were not so lucky, nor were Bull's skimmers.

The enemy has three platoons of combat cars for a total of 12 cars. Each car has an Ordnance value of 3. They attack using Chart B. The enemy withdraws after three rounds of combat.

The Slammers attack using Chart C.

If the Slammers are destroyed, turn to section 29.

If not, turn to section 39.

— 55 —

Small-arms fire from his skimmers kept the enemy infantry on their toes until Bull's tanks got across. Then the game became deadlier for the infantry. Bull's tanks lobbed round after round whenever an enemy fired on the skimmers. Shortly, Alpha India and Bravo India made the shore and dismounted to fight it out on foot. Bull assigned a tank to each infantry section. Farther north, Bull could tell that the initial surprise the enemy had been given when Smyth's platoon had supported Dyer's tanks had been overwhelming. Only sporadic gunfire could be heard from that direction. Finally the enemy quit the town and withdrew with what little force remained.

It had been a hard-fought battle, and gave Bull some moments worry for what the rest of the route would hold. Ahead of him lay a choice. He could head west toward phaseline Amber or he could lead his command to the village of Hillstart and north toward phaseline White, a crossroads where the route turned west to Regarra.

Record your casualties on the chart.

If Group Foxtrot heads west toward phaseline Amber, turn to section 74.

If Group Foxtrot heads north toward phaseline White, turn to section 75.

— 56 —

"This will be difficult, sir," Pete Smyth informed him. "I'd like permission to send my platoons in double echelon. Mine will approach Heatherlake from the east with another hidden in the woods to provide support. The third will face west to cross through the lake to the easternmost part of town. If your Tango elements could provide fire support from the southwest, firing northeastward, I think we could give any enemy a decent thrashing."

"Good," Bull agreed swiftly. Smyth really knows his tactics, Bull noted to himself. "Do it."

The slight whine of the small skimmers was soon lost as Bull's tanks jockeyed themselves into position. Bull waited tensely, aware that so much was in the hands of a man who still bore his scars. Pete Smyth's plan was a good one, but it required timing and control that might not be present in the training platoons he had to command.

"Foxtrot, Indias set," Smyth informed him in a quiet tone. It was that tone that told Bull his second-in-command was tense.

"Roger, Tangos are set. Proceed," Bull told him after a moment. He hated giving orders like that—orders that gave another man permission to be shot at or killed. Bull much preferred leading a battle himself, but this was one of those times when he had to give way to tactical necessity.

"Listen!" Ennis cried. "Shots!"

"I see them! From beyond the town!" Sara Engles added. "And there are more from in the town! Troops moving, too!"

"Have you got them sighted?" Bull asked Ennis.

"Roger," Ennis replied. "Say the word."

Bull put his knuckles to his teeth. There was the rub. When you gave another man charge of the battle, you let him give the orders. But what if Pete Smyth was dead? What then? Bull scarcely noticed that his teeth were leaving marks in his fingers.

The enemy have two platoons of infantry (eight squads). Each squad has an Ordnance value of 1. The enemy attacks using Chart D. Because of limited ammunition and nerve, the enemy only exchanges three volleys with the Slammers, then the enemy survivors withdraw.

Lieutenant Bromley's combined command attacks using Chart B.

If Combat Group Foxtrot destroys or routes the enemy, turn to section 59.

If the enemy destroys Combat Group Foxtrot, turn to section 29.

— 57 —

"Sir, we'll be annihilated!" Smyth cried. "If we cross in the open, any sort of heavy fire will destroy both platoons! And I don't give Bravo a better chance coming through the forest—it's too obvious."

Bull felt his face turning hot. Smyth had been bad enough the night before, but this insolence went beyond rivalry to insubordination.

"Ennis!" Bull roared. "Sight on Lieutenant Smyth's skimmer!" Ennis gaped at him for a moment, then traversed the huge turret to point at the indicated skimmer.

"You'll do as ordered or be shot on the spot," Bull told him in a firm voice. "Have you lost your nerve as well as everything else?"

"No sir," Smyth replied calmly. "I shall execute your orders. However, I want my protest placed on record."

"I wouldn't have it otherwise," Bull agreed coldly. "Move out." To Dyer he added, "Prepare to render aid as needed."

The three skimmer platoons grouped briefly, then spread out in a disorderly mass, reminding Bull of a stirred-up hornet's nest. Shortly, they began to line up at the side of the lake. Bravo India had already disappeared into the forest, charging gamely toward its destination.

Pete Smyth swore to himself. It *was* suicide! Murder,

really. Murder by Bromley. His tanks could never zero in tight enough on dug-in infantry. The enemy would have a field day as his skimmers tried to survive the flatness of the lake. Then, if they got through that, they would have to tackle that same infantry, ready and waiting for them.

"Move out," Smyth said over his command net.

They had scarcely got more than a third of the way across the lake when the enemy started firing on them. The first volley was a line of buzzbombs to force the hovertanks behind them to dodge, thus removing any hope of supporting fire. Intermingled with the flying bombs was small-arms fire directed at the skimmers. Shot after shot tore through his ranks. A burning skimmer swerved and collided with another skimmer, swamping it and throwing its crew into the water where their heavy equipment would sink them. It was a disaster!

The enemy has two platoons (eight squads) of infantry. They have surprised Combat Group Foxtrot and attack using Chart A. Because of ammunition shortages, however, they fight for only three rounds, then withdraw and have an Ordnance value of 2.

The disorganized Group Foxtrot attacks using Chart C.

If the enemy succeeds in wiping out Group Foxtrot, turn to section 29.

If Group Foxtrot forces the enemy to withdraw or destroys the enemy, turn to section 58.

— 58 —

It was a bloodbath. The skimmers lost over a squad in the first engagement. Bull's panzers were helpless from their position to render any more than minimal aid. The skimmers finally made it to the city, only to be picked off piecemeal by a well-entrenched enemy.

Desperately, Bull ordered the two tank platoons across. Their arrival diverted the enemy and allowed the shattered skimmer platoons to recover themselves somewhat. Bull's infantry pressed the attack, and the panzers followed it up, targeting building after building.

Finally it ended. Heatherlake was a shambles. Bromley's unit was badly bloodied and weakened by the encounter. Bull was furious. Furious with himself. Smyth had been right.

"Pete—" Bull began.

"Save it," Smyth replied harshly. "Tell it to the dead!"

Bull pursed his lips. He had to think, they had to move on. "Sierra Mike, you may occupy Green."

"Pretty copping red, isn't it?" the sergeant major returned angrily.

Bull had to continue. He had made a mistake, a bad one. They had survived mostly due to the tenacity of the Slammer infantry. He couldn't afford to make another mistake. Now he had to decide which way to go: north through Hillstart, toward phaseline White, or west as planned to the town of Tooey, phaseline Amber.

Record your casualties on the chart.

If Group Foxtrot heads west toward phaseline Amber, turn to section 74.

If group Foxtrot heads north toward phaseline White, turn to section 75.

— 59 —

Smyth's plan worked like a charm. The enemy, reacting to the small-arms fire from the skimmers, gave away its position and fell like easy meat to the Slammer tanks. Bull's tanks were able to perform surgery on the infested town, leveling only those buildings containing the enemy. Still, the result was disastrous for the city of Heatherlake. Huge skyscrapers had been tumbled by the bolts of energy from Bull's powerguns, while others leaned drunkenly against each other as if recovering from hangover.

His skimmers had taken their losses as well. Once the enemy had recovered from the initial shock, they had fought well enough, even if outnumbered.

Watching the smoke rising from distant points, and hearing the scream of civilian ambulances, Bull wondered what the full price had been and what the butcher's bill would be for the rest of the route to the wreck. It was his job to keep it small. Both civilian and military casualties had to be light. If his force succeeded in rescuing the Slammers at the expense of their clients, the repurcussions could be too great for Colonel Hammer to survive. Which way to go now?

He had planned to head west toward the town of Tooey, but now he wondered if he should head north through the town of Hillstart and toward phaseline White, a crossroads due east of Regarra.

Record your casualties on the chart.

If Group Foxtrot heads west toward phaseline Amber, turn to section 74.

If Group Foxtrot heads north toward phaseline White, turn to section 75.

— 60 —

"Tanks?" Bull asked aloud.

"That's my opinion," Smyth ventured.

"About a platoon," the Bravo India leader confirmed.

Bull cleared his throat and started to speak, but pulled himself short—he had placed Smyth in command. "What do you propose?" Bull asked him.

"With your permission, sir, I should like to send one of your tank platoons around the right flank to be led into an attack by Bravo India's scouts. The other platoon would come down the road—"

"—like rats in a trap," Bull noted.

"At the exact time when we believe that the platoon on the road will be detected, the infantry platoons will commence harassing fire," Smyth went on. "As soon as the enemy tanks have engaged the platoon on the road, the other tank platoon will engage the enemy from the rear."

"Good plan," Bull told him. "My platoon gets the road, Tango Alpha goes around."

"Sir!" Dyer protested.

"Shut up!" Bull snapped. "Well?" he asked Smyth.

"I have to agree with you, sir," Pete Smyth responded.

"Very well," Bull replied. "If I fall, you are in command."

Pete Smyth's pause was more than a second. "Yes sir," he replied. "When you're ready."

"Roger," Bull agreed. "Lariat Two, this is Two Six," Bull said to his platoon. "We're going into a trap. Alpha Tango is going to fire up their rear, but we get to spring the trap. Be on the lookout, and remember, you don't get paid until the end of the month!" He paused. "Move out!" To Smyth he said, "We're on our way!"

The four tanks of Foxtrot Tango spread themselves on either side of the road, cautious, yet displaying no more than the normal caution of a tank platoon moving through wooded terrain. Bull's tank was on the center right, Gleeson's to the right, Sam Lewis to the left, and Sergeant Healey on the far left. Four tanks against four hovertanks was no match. Four tanks hull down with their sights ready at close range in the woods was a death trap, and it didn't matter how much iridium armor a hovertank had. Bull was depending on two things: that the scouts of Bravo India could lead Dyer's tanks into position without giving them away, and that the harassing fire of the infantry platoons would scare and unsettle the enemy so much that it couldn't execute its trap quick enough to snuff out Bromley's platoon.

"We've contacted the scouts," Dyer relayed, mainly to comfort the first lieutenant. "They're pretty good," he added.

"This is Alpha India, coming up on the far edge of the forest," Peyton relayed.

"This is Tango. We are closing to six hundred meters," Bull told his command. "Three hundred meters," he told them a moment later.

Sweat poured down his back. Suddenly a shot rang. It wasn't a main gun but small-arms fire Bull heard ahead of them, but he wasn't sure from where. Were the scouts discovered? Were they ambushed? Had Bravo's platoon leader failed to detect screening infantry?

"One hundred meters," Bull relayed. A roar and a flash of

lightning burst from the undergrowth. "Dodge it, Timmons!" To Smyth he said, "We're under fire!"

Roll two six-sided dice.

If the result is less than or equal to the skimmers' Stealth value of 8, turn to section 76.

If the total rolled is greater than a Stealth value of 8, turn to section 77.

— 61 —

"There's nothing there," Smyth decided after a moment's glance.

"Keep your men on the lookout, though," Bull told him.

"Roger," Smyth replied.

The march continued. Bull relaxed; he could see the edge of the forest. Just as his tank started accelerating toward it, following in the wake of Smyth's infantry, four bright bolts burst from the woods ahead. One of them hit a skimmer in front of him and spattered the remains of the vehicle and its occupants against his tank. Again and again the enemy tanks roared. In vain Bull tried to home in on their positions, but the streaks of light that the powergun bolts made were gone in an instant, and the afterimage wavered in the eyes until the shots could have come from anywhere.

"Charge!" Bull roared, knowing that it was the only way out of the well-laid ambush. "Skimmers, get out of the way!" They were only fodder to the enemy tanks.

The enemy is attacking from a hull-down position in well-camouflaged areas. The four enemy tanks have Ordnance values of 2 each and attack using Chart B. The enemy engages for three rounds and then withdraws.

Combat Group Foxtrot, disorganized and rattled by the sudden ambush, rally to attack using Chart D.

If Group Foxtrot is destroyed, turn to section 29.

If Group Foxtrot survives, turn to section 78.

— 62 —

As they turned the final bend, Pete Smyth swore, "Via! We've got a platoon of tanks ahead!"

"Get off the road!" Bull roared to the infantry. "Circle to the north and be ready to support our fire." To his panzers he said, "Tango elements advance at quarter speed. Keep your eyes peeled; we're going to ambush an ambush."

At quarter speed the huge tanks made little noise. Bull ordered the infantry to start firing. The distraction allowed his tanks to approach without being heard. The skill of his drivers and tank commanders allowed his platoons to approach without being seen.

"There they are!" Ennis cried. "Just having a good ol' shoot-up!"

"We'll break the party up!" Bull replied. "Tango and Tango Alpha, engage!"

Eight guns burst over the noise of small-arms fire from the infantry and the sporadic bursts of the four guns of the enemy tanks. Eight guns fired eight lances of flaming death at four targets. Then the targets started firing back.

The enemy has four tanks, each of Ordnance value 2. They were distracted by the infantry and slow to recover, but they have not failed to give the infantry a rough ride. The enemy attacks using Chart D.

The Slammers, having engaged with their infantry first, have endangered the small but agile skimmer-mounted foot soldiers. On the other hand, the huge panzers attacked an exposed flank and exploited surprise. The Slammers attack using Chart B.

The enemy fights for three rounds, and then the enemy survivors withdraw.

If Group Foxtrot is destroyed, turn to section 29.

If the enemy is destroyed or withdraws, turn to section 79.

— 63 —

He wasn't careful enough. Just as his tanks were advancing to close the gap with the infantry, the roar of four powerguns in front of him announced that the pongoes had met more than their match. Bull swore; they were just about out of this forest to boot!

"Anyone got a sighting on them?" he asked.

"Negative. Not a sign—just the bursts. They've got some of my men," Bravo India's platoon leader said sourly.

"All India elements veer off the road, ground in the forest!" Bull yelled. "All Tango elements charge!"

It was a desperate move, pitting the speed of his hovertanks against the aim of an enemy hull down and camouflaged. "You pongoes keep your heads down!"

The enemy has four tanks with an Ordnance value of 2 each. The enemy fights for three rounds, using Chart B, and then withdraws.

Combat Group Foxtrot fights at a disadvantage. The hovertanks are charging into fire without knowing their targets, and the skimmers have been forced to ground, allowing them to put up only token fire. Group Foxtrot attacks using Chart D.

If Group Foxtrot is destroyed, turn to section 29.

If the enemy withdraws or is defeated, turn to section 79.

— 64 —

Greer's squad was the worst hit. Bull feared that he would be cleaning bits of that squad out from the insides of his tank for the next week and knew that he would never forget the way they had died. His Slammers had recovered well, though, and had given as good as they had got. The enemy were all dead or in retreat.

"Regroup, wounded to Victor," Bull mumbled wearily over the radio, wiping his forehead with his scarf and jumping at the sight of blood. It wasn't his own—someone from Greer's squad. He threw the scarf over the side of the tank.

"Anyone got a toothpick?" Timmons quipped.

"I'll shove one down your throat," Ennis growled.

"Victor Niner Zero, can you spare some men for Charlie?" Bull asked on the sergeant major's own frequency, hoping not to be overheard by Bravo India's badly shaken commander.

"On the way," the sergeant major replied with feeling. "They fought well."

"They had to," the voice of Lieutenant Smyth agreed.

"Will they hold?" Bull asked his second-in-command.

"Sure," Smyth replied instantly. "They're Slammers, aren't they?"

"Mike Two Zero, Charlie Niner Zero, ready to move," Bravo India's young platoon leader called.

"Roger, Charlie. Well done," Bull replied feelingly. Bravo India was ready to move. Bull was itching to finish the job and now had to figure out how.

If Bull decides to position the skimmers in front of the tanks, turn to section 51.

If he decides to send his tanks to recon ahead of the rest of his command, turn to section 54.

— 65 —

"Leave the wounded for Victor Niner Zero," Bull finished. He noted with relief that there weren't too many wounded this time. The skimmers moved out, making a wide and quick approach to the next phaseline. Sergeant Greer's squad of Bravo India made the final approach. He had just reached the outskirts of the town when withering fire sliced his squad to bits.

"Pull back!" Bull shouted. "November Niner Zero, advance!" To his platoon he yelled, "Fire!"

Buzzbombs roared out of the city toward Dyer's advancing tanks. Peyton's platoon had grounded on the west of the town and was advancing with difficulty on foot. Smyth's platoon was busily extricating itself from Dyer's advancing tanks and the confusion that was Bravo India.

The enemy has two infantry squads in the town. Each squad has an Ordnance value of 1. The enemy has surprised the Slammers in the open and attacks using Chart A.

The Slammers are surprised but respond well. They attack using Chart B.

If the Slammers are destroyed, turn to section 29.

If the enemy is defeated or withdraws, turn to section 64.

— 66 —

"Whiskey Three Yankee Niner Zero Alpha," Bull provided helpfully.

"Yes?" Engles replied in confusion. Then she turned to her lieutenant, scowling, and called, "Bravo Two Victor Niner

Zero, Whiskey Three Yankee Niner Zero Alpha. Radio check, over.''

"Bravo Two Victor Niner Zero. Roger, out,'' The sergeant major replied. Engles very pointedly glared admonition at her commander.

"Leave your wounded with Victor Niner Zero, Juliet,'' Bull amended.

Turn to section 65.

— 67 —

It was short. It was sharp. It was over as suddenly as it had begun. Foxtrot's panzers fired, but there was nothing to aim at. The firing ceased, and the air slowly filled with the cries of wounded and the last curses of the dying. A strange hideous smell—a mixture of dirt, metal, burnt flesh, and torn atoms—spread across the battlefield. The enemy had either withdrawn after their first few rounds or been blown to fragments.

"Okay, how many did you get?'' Bull asked Sergeant Gleeson.

"I don't know!'' Gleeson swore. "I honestly don't know!''

The combat group continued through the forest and toward the crossroads. While Bull chided Gleeson for not keeping better count of his kills, he pondered over how to move through the next section of terrain. At the crossroads they would turn left and head through wide open plains to phaseline Gold. After that came Iridium.

If Lieutenant Bromley decides to keep his tanks in front, with the infantry close behind, turn to section 68.

If he chooses to send his infantry out in a far recon ahead of his panzers and the softskinneds, turn to section 69.

— 68 —

"We need speed," Bull decided aloud. "Mike, this is Two Zero. Tanks first. Golf on the left, November on the right. Alpha, Bravo, Charlie left to right following. Victor to follow when the terrain's cleared. Move out!"

The tanks roared forward, pressing the grasses flat with their weight but not transmitting the dips of the terrain to their passengers as they rode on their great cushions of air. They moved out, a hundred meters between each tank and a platoon on either side of the road. Behind them, closer together, came the skimmers.

"More speed!" Bull roared, feeling the press of time. He put his binoculars to his eyes and scanned the terrain ahead, hoping to catch the first glimpse of the town codenamed phaseline Gold. It seemed forever, but then a dark smudge on the horizon to the north attracted his attention: the wreck of the transport *Vindictive*. Occasional bright flares of light licked out, and he knew that some Slammers were still fighting for their survival.

"Faster!" Bull snapped. "I've got Iridium in sight!" They were halfway to Gold. They were going to make it.

Four bolts of thick cyan energy licked across the plain from the forest to the left, followed instantly by four more from the right, and then to top it off, a barrage of small-arms fire from the town ahead told Bull that he was in for one more fight.

The enemy has two platoons of hovertanks and one platoon of skimmer-mounted infantry. The eight tanks have Ordnance values of 4 each, and the four skimmer squads have Ordnance values of 2 each. The Slammers are surprised and trapped, so the enemy attacks using Chart B. They cease fire after three rounds, when they run out of ammunition.

The Slammers attack using Chart D.

If the Slammers are defeated, turn to section 29.

If the Slammers survive, turn to section 32.

— 69 —

"Mike, this is Mike Two Zero," Bull called to his command. "Juliet elements will take the lead with sectional reinforcement of Yankee elements. Juliet elements will perform far recon, paying particular attention to any cover. Golf Two Four and Tree Six will remain with the Victor elements."

"Roger," Smyth agreed, adding, "Request assignments."

"Roger. November Niner Zero, your first section goes to Charlie Niner Zero. You have command," Bull told Dyer. "Your second section goes to Bravo Niner Zero." To Sergeant Lewis he said, "Gulf One Four, you go with Alpha Niner Zero."

"Roger," Dyer acknowledged. Lewis's reply came on his heels.

"Move out," Bull ordered. Lewis's section broke away and took up station with Lieutenant Peyton's platoon, which was arrayed on the left flank. Dyer's section split off with Bravo India while Dyer's second section moved due west with Smyth. They cleared the foothills to the left and right and fanned out, Peyton south toward the lake and the forest beyond, Dyer and Bravo India to the right and the west.

Bull was glad that he had chosen this formation. With the critical softskinneds tied to the road, any attack could rake and destroy them, leaving the survivors of the wrecked transport without food, medicine, and, most important, ammunition. The three far-flung infantry platoons teamed with the tank sections could speak with authority in any situation they found while awaiting support from the rest of Group Foxtrot.

On the left flank Peyton's command veered south sharply after they cleared the foothills and reached the forest before the head of the lake. Leaving a small force on the near side of the lake; Peyton took the main bulk of his troops close and into the forest, skirting or snooping into them as he continued west toward the next foothill.

On the right flank Dyer's command headed north for the small woods and cleared it quickly, pincering the lake on the way to the next forest west. Dyer's command was making better time over more open ground than Peyton's, but Smyth was keeping in line with both flanks.

It was getting near the time when Bull could move out with the softskinneds. He brought his binoculars up and tried to resolve the details of the distant town that was phaseline Gold. To the north, behind it, he thought he saw smoke, but he couldn't be certain.

If you have "Smyth" written on a piece of paper, turn to 111.

If you have not written "Smyth," turn to section 38.

— 70 —

Even with the threat the enemy posed, Bull's panzers dealt with them easily. The skimmers took some damage, and Bull's armor did not come away unscathed, but the enemy was no serious threat to his mission. The Slammers passed through the woods and on to the crossroad where they would turn left toward Regarra and the beleaguered survivors of the wrecked transport. They left the cries of their wounded enemy for the following softskinneds, and left the pall of dust and debris that rose into the air as a grim warning to any who stood in their path.

The terrain was open between the crossroad and the next phaseline. Bull debated which formation to use.

If Bull chooses to keep his command tightly bunched, with the hovertanks in the front and the skimmers close behind, turn to section 68.

If Bull chooses to send his skimmers in a far-flung recon ahead of his main body, turn to section 69.

— 71 —

The minutes ticked by. Bull glanced at the sun for a moment as it bore heavily down on his tanks. There was a lot to be said for just being an enlisted man: wait for orders and follow them. It was different being in command of several elements—worse, having to give command to another. Nothing worried Bull Bromley more than the thought of men dying because he'd guessed wrong about another man. Nothing except getting those men killed all by himself.

"Tango, India. Contact." Smyth's voice was a whisper. "I've got four tanks on the hill to the east of the pass."

"Add a platoon of infantry in the woods to the west," Peyton added calmly.

"Damn!" Bull swore. "Could I send tanks to you, Pete?"

"Negative, this is prime billy-goat country," Smyth replied. "These guys came up from the road and they're dug in, hull down."

"They're not moving, at least," Peyton remarked.

"Can I get to them?" Bull asked.

"Not from where you are," Smyth replied. "You'd have to come into their line of sight, and they'd have you before you'd have them."

Bull stopped himself from hitting the hard iridium of his tank in frustration. It would only hurt like hell, he told himself. "What about those grunts?" he asked Peyton.

"You've got to come around the bend, sir, before you'll get to them." Peyton replied. "But sir . . ."

"Go ahead," Bull allowed. Sergeant, now Lieutenant, Peyton had always had ideas.

"We, Alpha and Bravo, could start an attack on this platoon. Then you could maneuver in the confusion and take on the tanks." Peyton sketched his plan. "It would have to be fast, and it wouldn't be much of a distraction, but it's what we've got."

"I could assault the tanks from the rear. They've got their hatches open," Smyth offered.

"No way," Bull declined flatly. "We're going to use your

plan, Peyton. Pete, you'll force those guys to keep their heads down the minute my tanks get in the open. I don't want your guys hurt. We can't replace 'em.''

"Okay," Smyth agreed.

"This'll be timed," Bull added. "Peyton, your attack begins in two minutes. The tanks will move out in three minutes. Smyth, you'll start harassing fire in three and a half minutes. Understood?''

"Roger," Smyth and Peyton agreed together.

"Dyer?" Bull asked.

"Got you."

"Roger," Bravo India's platoon leader added.

"Lariat, we move in two," Bull told his platoon. "We've got tanks on the hill to the east and infantry in the woods just around the bend ahead. We're going for the tanks. Be ready; they've got the drop on us.''

Two minutes are one hundred twenty seconds long. The reaction time of a human in good shape is about a thirtieth of a second. Three thousand six hundred reactions later, Bull heard the sharp report of small-arms fire away to the northeast.

Alpha India and Bravo India had engaged the infantry. Less than six hundred reactions later, Bull jumped at the sound of powerguns as they lanced down the hill toward his infantry. For the next twelve hundred reactions Bull winced every time an enemy powerbolt forked out from the mountain into his attacking infantry below. Peyton and Bravo's leaders were too engrossed in the battle to give him a report—or they were dead already. Finally, eternity ended.

"Move out!" The command came from somewhere deep in Bull, from the part of him that hated war, hated the killing, and hated worst of all any of his men having to die. "Gun it! Get those blowers rolling, dammit! We've got some grunts to save!''

As though they all felt the same anger at having to wait and watch while their buddies took such a beating, the eight tanks of Bull Bromley's panzers shot forward on either side of the road. Ahead, on the mountain, the lightning lances of death wavered and stopped as the enemy detected this new threat.

Then thunder rained on them. Above that, from behind the mountain, what appeared to be a shower of blue-green meteors roared toward the enemy's tanks: Smyth's platoon hailing death on the unwary.

The enemy has a platoon of infantry made up of four squads (each Ordnance value 1) in the forest. Dug in on the mountain is a platoon of four tanks, each with an Ordnance value of 2. The enemy has been surprised twice and attacks using Chart C. They fight for three rounds and then withdraw because of a morale problem.

The Slammers, attacking against a well-placed position with little cover, have made the best of their situation and maneuvered to their advantage. They attack using Chart B.

If the enemy destroys Combat Group Foxtrot, turn to section 29.

If the enemy withdraws or is destroyed, turn to section 80.

— 72 —

The waiting was the worst of it. Bull could take battle; you either lived through it or you didn't. At the end of it all, your nerves caught up with you and you shook. It didn't matter who you were. Even the sadists shook (but not with fear). Now, Bull waited. It could be nothing, no enemy, no trouble. Maybe those two tanks were it—the end of Jebbitt's Raiders. Bull snorted, thinking: no way! Waiting was bad; waiting to see if someone else would die or screw up was impossible.

"India, report," Bull said as calmly as he could.

"We're almost on the western end. Nothing yet," Smyth replied softly. Bull could tell that he was feeling the strain. At least he was moving, going someplace.

"Alpha India, report," Bull said to Peyton.

"We're going west around the western hill and we'll enter the forest shortly," Peyton responded.

"What about Bravo India?" Bull asked.

"We're heading west around the other hill," Bravo's platoon leader replied.

"I told you to stay put!" Peyton yelled, but Bull didn't hear it. All he heard was the sudden roar of four tanks as they blazed down on the unsuspecting infantry platoon from the mountain to the east. Sharper sounds and smaller bolts told Bull that a platoon in the woods to the west had also found Bravo India.

"Peyton, go around!" Bull ordered. "Smyth, keep those tanks busy!" To his own command he said one word: "Charge!"

The enemy has skillfully hidden themselves on both the mountain to the east and the woods to the west of the road. They had detected Bravo India and are now decimating it. The casualties must be first four units of infantry.

The enemy has four tanks, each of strength 2 and four squads of infantry, each of strength 1. The enemy attacks using Chart C. The enemy will only fire for three rounds, then withdraw. Total their attack strengths and alternate bases.

The Slammers have been caught in the lurch. Lieutenant Bromley's orders give them a chance to recover. They attack on Chart E.

If the Slammers are destroyed, turn to section 29.

If the enemy withdraws or the Slammers destroy them, turn to section 80.

— 73 —

The roar of guns from the second quarter caught the enemy unaware, and they were confused. Bull's panzers poured round after round into them. Slowly the enemy split its forces to respond to Bull's new menace. A few ill-directed rounds flared toward him, then the enemy got their range and started firing in earnest.

The enemy has four hovertanks, each with an Ordnance value of 4. They are surprised and confused and attack using Chart D. The enemy withdraws after three rounds of combat.

The Slammers attack using Chart B.

If the enemy destroys the Slammers, turn to section 29.

If the enemy withdraws or is destroyed, turn to section 70.

— 74 —

"Foxtrot, we're going on to Amber," Bull told his command. The question, as always, was how? The terrain to Amber was pretty open. It was blitzkrieg terrain: the terrain where "lightning war" really could happen. The trouble was, it was suited also for Bull's skimmer-mounted infantry. He could let his tanks roam far ahead and clear out any trouble, or let the skimmers loose to comb the terrain over and above. With their small silhouette and agility, the skimmers could dodge most trouble they met and report back to the tanks. If the tanks roamed ahead, there would be little chance of protecting the softskinneds if an enemy got around them. If the skimmers went ahead, they would have little chance against a well-positioned defense, especially if there were tanks.

If Bull chooses to lead his tanks forward in recon, turn to section 83.

If he chooses to send the infantry afield in a skimmer recon, turn to section 84.

— 75 —

"Foxtrot, we're going north," Bull informed his command. "Regroup, and get your wounded over to the softskinneds. Alpha India, detail two men to scout."

"Roger," Peyton replied.

As Bull's panzer whined through the streets of Heatherlake, he struggled to consider his next move. Foxtrot would head due north, through Hillstart and Gold City, veer west at phaseline White and head for Regarra and the survivors. The terrain got tricky coming up to White, and was not the best throughout the route. Bull was torn between sending his skimmers forward in a recon or having them close behind with his tanks as a shield.

What should Bull do?

If he keeps his skimmers close behind his tanks, turn to section 85.

If he sends his skimmers on recon, turn to section 86.

— 76 —

"We have engaged the enemy!" Dyer exclaimed on the heels of Bull's words. All around Bull the woods erupted in the sound of small-arms fire and the roaring of the tanks' main guns. Bolts of intense white light that could boil away the thickest armor hurled themselves toward Bull and his tanks. It was going to be a hot, short battle.

The enemy has four tanks, each of Ordnance value 2. They fight using Chart E. The enemy is surrounded and fights until completely destroyed.

Combat Group Foxtrot fights using Chart B.

If Group Foxtrot is destroyed, turn to section 29.

If Group Foxtrot defeats the enemy, turn to section 78.

— 77 —

"Dammit, they've spotted us!" Dyer yelled. "Engage! Engage! Engage!"

A roar of powerguns burst the air, and Bull was startled to see twin bolts of lightning streak toward his tank. "Dodge!" Bull cried, too late. Moving at the speed of light, both bolts struck his tank and rocked it. On either side the glancing blows scored the iridium hull, leaving steaming streaks of molten metal in their wake. Bull's own gun roared back, its sound blending with the rest of his platoon firing blindly in front of them.

The enemy has four tanks, each of Ordnance value 2. The enemy fights using Chart D. They are surrounded and will fight until completely destroyed.

Group Foxtrot, disorganized but fighting, attacks using Chart C.

If Group Foxtrot is destroyed, turn to section 29.

If the enemy is destroyed, turn to section 78.

— 78 —

The biggest difference between winning and losing a battle was that the living had to put up with the smell of dead flesh. Sometimes Bull thought smelling that stench was the only way to know that he was still alive. Ahead of them were four slag heaps. One of them had been a tank that tried to get away but had the bad luck to be Sam Lewis's chance to win a third case of beer.

In the afterimages that still burned in his mind, Bull could remember that the enemy had fought well. At least two of his tanks bore scars to remind them of this encounter. Skimmers had been hit, too, although Bull didn't have a full report yet on the damage to men and machines.

"We're ready for casualties; pass them back here!" Sergeant Major Ogren ordered.

"Roger," Bull agreed. "Foxtrot, let's get those casualties back to Sierra Major and get out of here!"

"You just leave it to us foxes, and we'll do some serious trotting," Sergeant Healey intoned.

"There are some grounds on which a tank crew could lose a case of beer, Sergeant," Bull reminded him lightly.

"Lariat Two Four, roger," Healey acknowledged. In an undertone he added, "That'll still leave us with a warehouse full."

"Foxtrot, India. We've crossed the stream and are continuing." Pete Smyth's voice reminded Bull of their mission.

"Roger. Alpha India, Bravo India, status?" Bull asked.

"Alpha India on the move, approaching the stream," Peyton replied.

"Bravo India . . ." Bravo India's leader hesitated. "Moving now, sir."

"Don't take too much time," Bull replied lightly. He would have to watch that platoon carefully.

"We're in the woods," Smyth told him.

"We're going around," Peyton added.

"Just coming to the hill now," Bravo India reported.

"Hold it!" Bravo's leader was shrill. "India, spot report—infantry in the woods just in front of you!"

"Roger. India ground!" Smyth said to his platoon. "Peyton, get behind them. Tango and Alpha Tango, ground."

Bull bridled when he heard the order, but Pete Smyth was the commander on the spot and Bull knew to respect him. Dyer did not. "What's he going on about?" the new officer questioned. "Why the—"

"Quiet!" Bull ordered. He glanced at Sara to see if Pete Smyth had overheard Dyer's remarks, but she shook her head. They must have been on the tank company's frequency.

"Foxtrot, request permission to launch infantry support," Smyth said shortly.

"How are you going to execute it?" Bull asked. He did not need to add: your force is surrounding that platoon, and if you all open fire, your stray shots will hit our own men.

"Bravo India will stage a mock assault from the hill,"

Smyth began quietly. "This will allow Alpha India to get into position. At my mark, Alpha India and India will assault in a wedge. At that time Bravo India will withdraw from the hill and regroup. The panzers will take position on the hill and finish the enemy off. Bravo India will be in reserve."

"Go for it," Bull replied. The plan depended on Peyton's platoon getting into position without being spotted. If they were spotted, and the enemy commander was good enough . . . Bull didn't want to think about it.

Be sure to record any casualties from the last battle, then roll two six-sided dice.

If the result is equal to or less than the infantry's Stealth value of 8, turn to section 89.

If the result is greater than 8, turn to section 90.

— 79 —

The fire was intense, but it was futile. With only four tanks against four hovertanks, the end was predictable. What could not be predicted was how many of Bromley's skimmers and tanks the enemy would destroy before they withdrew.

In the heat of the battle Bull Bromley did not think of such things. He roared out the orders and tried not to wince as skimmers were raked by fire from the tank's turret tribarrel. Beside him a powergun bolt, pure energy, tore into the side of Gleeson's Lariat Two Eight. Bull swore as his eyes recovered from the sight, and he yelled when he saw that Two Eight had caught the blow at an angle. It was a badly scored tank, but still fighting; its next shot took out the attacker.

"Way to go, Two Eight!" Timmons whooped.

Suddenly the shooting was one-sided. The enemy was either destroyed or had withdrawn. "Cease fire. Good shooting," Bull told his tanks.

"Case of beer!" Gleeson yelled back.

"Done," Bull replied.

It's cheaper, on the emotions at least, than writing letters, he thought to himself. Funny thing about mercenaries; they still had people who had to be notified when they got killed. Bull never liked writing those letters and remembered an ancient saying: "Say what you like, it'll only break their hearts." This time he didn't have to break too many hearts.

"Get those ambulances up here!" Bull roared to the sergeant major. "I want the wounded out of here and this unit moving again."

To his second in command Bull said, "Smyth, let me know when you're moving." To his own platoon he added, "Good work, guys—but don't get cocky! We're moving out as soon as these pongoes finish changing their drawers." Somebody snickered at his rude remark.

Moments later the convoy moved forward. They left the forest and entered a wide clearing. To their right was a small hill, and ahead was a woods into which the road plunged once more.

Shaken by the onslaught, the skimmers moved cautiously, stopping to peer ahead before moving on in sections or even squads. Bull champed at the delay but knew he couldn't force them to go faster without rattling some of the recruits beyond battle readiness. Sure, Slammers were recruited from tough outfits, but even tough outfits had horse sense and the fear given any man who hopes to see the next day. It was no surprise to Bull when, as they rounded a corner over a stream and headed toward the forest, one of the skimmers spotted something.

"Sir! On the hill behind us, we think we've spotted a tank," Bravo India's leader said nervously.

"Let me have a look," Bull said. The image was quickly relayed to Bull's viewer. Sure enough, there was something odd there. But what was tanks, or simply fallen trees?

If Lieutenant Bromley acts on this reconnaissance, turn to section 87.

If he decides to press on, turn to section 88.

— 80 —

The next minutes were a montage of dirt flying, trees falling, and earth being leveled, backed by a cacophony of guns exploding and men screaming out pain, imprecations, orders, and commands. Peyton's platoon decisively engaged the enemy infantry and assaulted them so fiercely that the infantry routed. On the hill the enemy tanks fired without the precision they needed to create a victory but with enough skill to leave skimmers disabled, tanks scored, and men dead. When the firing stopped, Bull wasn't sure whether the enemy tanks had been destroyed, buried under rubble, or withdrawn. He didn't care. It was over for now.

"Foxtrot, Sierra Mike will handle casualties. Get them back to him as quickly as possible." On Pete Smyth's frequency he said, "Pete, when can you move?"

"We'll be ready in two minutes," Lieutenant Smyth responded. "You want me to take the van?"

"That's right. I want Peyton on your right and Bravo on your left."

Two minutes later the first of India platoon's skimmers headed down either side of the road through the narrow pass between woods and mountain. On their tail the van of Lieutenant Peyton's Alpha India swung to the right to scour the forest behind the mountain and cross over the road northward to nose about two hills on the way back.

Bravo India was a bit slower in getting off the mark but made up for it, sticking its head into the end of the woods to the left and then around the long hill that lay beside their path.

Group Foxtrot cleared the first fork, turning to the left to follow the road westward. Alpha India pronounced the hill to the north clear on both sides, while Pete Smyth's India platoon checked the base of the mountain straight ahead.

Bravo India was peeking into the forest that bracketed the road to Gold City when the call came.

"Contact. One enemy infantry platoon in the woods to your southwest," Bravo's platoon leader said.

"I think I've got something else; I'm not sure," Peyton said on the heels of Bravo's leader. "It's to the north of us, in the woods after the fork. Might be infantry."

"Let's see," Bull said. Instantly one of his consoles displayed the site Lieutenant Peyton was examining.

"That's full magnification," Peyton explained before Bull could ask.

Examine the picture.

If you believe there is something there, turn to section 91.

If you believe Lieutenant Bromley should not worry about this report, turn to section 92.

— 81 —

"Bull!" a voice jeered. "Bull Bromley. More like bullock! We've got you now!"

The enemy has monitored your communications and is ready for you. They have four hovertanks, each with an Ordnance value of 4. They attack using Chart C and withdraw, because of a shortage of ammunition, after three rounds of combat.

The Slammers also attack using Chart C.

If the enemy destroys Combat Group Foxtrot, turn to section 29.

If the enemy withdraws or is destroyed, turn to section 70.

— 82 —

Bull's skimmers were good, especially with Pete Smyth in the lead. Some went far west, beyond the small hill on the left of the road and through the narrow forest, heading north. Others skirted the mountain north of phaseline Copper. Peyton's skimmers had the left flank and Bravo India the right.

"Contact!" Peyton called just as Bull was sure that the area was safe. "I have two . . . no, four enemy tanks in the woods on either side of the road!" he said. "They're just northeast of us. It's perfect for them. You come around the bend straight into the line of fire, with hills on either side. A nice death trap."

"Nasty," Smyth agreed. Bull examined Lieutenant Peyton's display on his third vision block and had to agree. He could just make out two hovertanks, obviously stolen from the wreck. The enemy had chosen a good position. He couldn't see the other two tanks.

"Where are the others?" Bull asked.

"Facing north," Peyton replied, chuckling. "Guess they didn't hear all the fighting."

"Very good!" Bull responded. "Here's what we'll do. We'll send a tank platoon around to you and open fire on them. When the firing starts, my platoon will head down the road and add to the confusion. The other skimmers will follow up behind me."

His words became actions. Five minutes later Dyer's platoon had made contact with Alpha India. In unison Dyer's platoon barraged the enemy positions, abetted by small-arms fire and an occasional buzzbomb from Peyton. The enemy responded, but poorly.

"Move out!" Bull roared to his command.

As his tanks roared around the corner toward the enemy and the firefight, Bull kept his binoculars up, ready to engage the first target he spotted.

If you have "Bluejay Five" written on a piece of paper, turn to section 73.

If you have not written "Bluejay Five," turn to section 81.

— 83 —

"Tango, Tango Alpha, we will recon by sections two kilometers in advance of the rest of the column," Bull said. "The infantry will form a wedge in front of the softskinneds. Move out!"

"Tango Alpha, roger," Dyer acknowledged, putting words into deeds as his four tanks broke into groups of two and headed west. Bull's own command also broke up. Sam Lewis's section moved almost due north. Lewis's section soon nudged about the edge of the forest to the north and proceeded on toward the marshes. Dyer's section examined the lake west of the town and continued on westward. Bull's own section stayed near the road, checking out farmhouses and the small dips and valleys along the way.

They had cleared the town and the skimmers were following when all hell broke lose behind them. Small arms buzzed at their rear and tore strips out of the skimmers.

"Turn around!" Bull roared, turning backward to peer behind them. In the forests to the northwest and northeast of Heatherlake, two enemy infantry platoons had opened fire on Bull's infantry. "Tango, Alpha Tango, fall back!" Bull ordered sharply.

"On the way!" Lewis replied, his two tanks racing back toward their beleaguered infantry, far ahead of Bull's following section. "Holy cow, they're using some of our skimmers!" Lewis exclaimed. "Bluejay Five! Bluejay Five! All Foxtrot—Bluejay Five. The bird has squawked."

If you have "Bluejay Five" written down on a piece of paper, turn to section 97.

If you don't, turn to section 98.

— 84 —

"Foxtrot, we will execute a reinforced infantry recon two kilometers ahead of the main body," Bull announced. "Alpha Tango Section One will escort Bravo India, Alpha Tango Section Two will escort Alpha India." He paused. He didn't want to keep his section with the softskinneds, but it was his duty. "Tango Section Two will escort India. India plus will follow the road, Alpha plus will take the north side, Bravo plus the south side."

"Roger," the platoon leaders acknowledged.

"You get to guard my hide!" Sergeant Major Ogren cackled. "Good work for you, too!"

"Request permission to recon north of Green," Peyton asked.

"Roger. You recon to the east; Bravo India take the west. All units will then pivot through ninety degrees to continue the march," Bull ordered. "Do it."

Peyton's Alpha was the first unit to move out, heading toward the woods that were to their right and would be dangerously behind them when they turned west. Pete Smyth's command charged off to the forest on their left. Both platoons headed toward their targets, while Bravo India checked out their route west.

Peyton's cry of "Contact!" was swallowed by the roar of two hovertanks as they loosed their main guns. As Bull watched, two bolts streaked across the plain and licked the forest. "Contact!" Smyth cried seconds later.

"Roger, what size?" Bull asked, adding, "All units support the action."

"I've got a platoon in the woods," Lieutenant Peyton replied.

"Make that two," Smyth added. Then, incredulously, "They've got our skimmers!"

"Bluejay Five! Bluejay Five!" Ogren screamed. "The bird has squawked! Bluejay Five!"

If you have "Bluejay Five" written on a piece of paper, turn to section 100.

If you did not write "Bluejay Five," turn to section 99.

— 85 —

"Tanks will move out first, skimmers'll follow," Bull told his command. "Alpha Tango will take the right flank, Tango the left. Alpha India will come up behind Alpha Tango, Bravo India behind Tango. India, you will form the van of the softskinneds and be in reserve. Move out now."

There was some jockeying as the panzers and pongoes moved themselves into the new marching order, but they had it sorted out a kilometer outside of Heatherlake. The road went west and then turned ninety degrees to curve east on the approach to Hillstart. There were two forests on the route, one close to the west side of the road and one separated from the road by a lake on the east.

"Tango and Alpha Tango, sniff out the forests," Bull ordered as they neared them. Dyer's detachment veered east to avoid the lake while Sam Lewis's section of Lariat Two charged straight for the western forest in the true spirit of Lightnin' Lewis. The assault paid off badly for Lewis when a buzzbomb arrowed straight for his tank. A quick jink by Lewis's gunner dodged the buzzbomb, but more were coming even before Lewis could exclaim, "Infantry platoon in the forest!"

"We've got one here, too!" Sergeant Biddle of Dyer's platoon added hastily. "They've got some of our skimmers!"

"Bluejay Five! Bluejay Five!" Lewis yelped. "The bird has squawked!"

If you have "Bluejay Five" written down on a piece of paper, turn to section 101.

If you did not write "Bluejay Five," turn to section 102.

— 86 —

"Smyth, I want a skimmer recon," Bull grunted. "You take the van. Put Bravo on your right and Alpha on your left. My tanks'll back you up." With the skimmers sniffing around the forest, Lieutenant Bromley was convinced that they would find any enemy before it found them. The skimmers would be able to call in accurate coordinates for the panzers to fire on and crush the enemy.

"Roger," Smyth replied. "Ready when you are."

"Move out."

"From left to right: Alpha India, India, Bravo India—move out!" Smyth barked.

"Alpha India, roger."

"Bravo India, roger."

Like gnats, the skimmers flitted off to the north. Like eagles, the huge hovertanks followed. Behind them the softskinned vehicles trailed along. Bull frowned when he saw Bravo India's skimmers peel off toward the upcoming forest. Looking northward, he saw nothing of Peyton's platoon as it made a similar approach to the other forest. Smyth, for all his faults, was invisible on either side of the road ahead, even when Bull switched to the infrared sights of his vision block.

The gunfire that erupted from Bravo India was not unexpected—a young platoon leader will fire at any suspicious movement—but the return volley from the forest was. Like fencing swords, foils of light flicked between the forest and the oncoming platoon.

"Report!" Bull demanded.

"A platoon of infantry, skimmer mounted, in the woods!" Bravo India's leader replied. "Request assistance."

"Skimmers?!" Bull exclaimed. "Jebbit doesn't have—" His words were cut off as a second volley, this time from the northern forest, licked out toward Bravo India. It was answered by the well-placed Alpha India.

"Skimmers in the woods!" Peyton exclaimed. "Bluejay Five! Bluejay Five! The bird has squawked!"

If you haven't written "Bluejay Five," turn to section 103.

If you have "Bluejay Five" written on a piece of paper, turn to section 104.

— 87 —

"Something there, all right," Smyth remarked quietly. "Looks like a pair of tanks at the least."

"I agree," Bull responded. "What are your suggestions?"

"Let the skimmers continue down the road toward the forest," Smyth replied quickly, "then have the tanks wheel right behind the hill and pummel the enemy while they're still trying to sight on the skimmers."

"Dangerous," Dyer remarked.

"Effective," Peyton countered.

"Do it," Bull ordered.

As the skimmers continued their forward prowling, the hovertanks gently veered more toward the hill. Bull strained for a better look at the enemy's position, but it was too well camouflaged—it really looked like fallen trees. Bull switched his binoculars to infrared and still couldn't make out the enemy. The skimmers were in position.

"Now!" Bull yelled. The hovertanks poured on a burst of speed, tearing around the hill with gunsights aligned on the camouflage. "Fire when ready!"

The roar of powerguns stung the air as the gleaming bolts of death leaped across the distance to tear the ground and rattle the form of the enemy. Only—

The sharp rattle of tribarrels pouring a staccato cacophony startled Bull for a moment. Then he realized it was coming from the other side of the hill!

"Enemy platoon in the woods!" Lieutenant Peter Smyth reported with an edge of horror in his voice. "They're ripping into Peyton! Request immediate assistance!"

Bull looked at his targets. The first barrage of powerguns had shown them to be nothing more than fallen trees! He cursed.

"Tango and Alpha Tango, charge the hill!" Bull roared to his tankers. "India, we're on the way!"

The enemy has a well-hidden platoon of infantry in the forest. They have surprised the Slammers. The platoon is composed of four squads, each of Ordnance value 2. They attack using Chart B and withdraw after three rounds of combat.

The Slammers are surprised. The tanks will not arrive in time to support the infantry; however, they will arrive in time to take casualties. The infantry must fight by itself using Chart D. Losses are taken from the infantry first, then the tanks if there is no infantry left. The tanks can only fight after all the infantry are lost.

If the Slammers are destroyed, turn to section 29.

If the Slammers survive the attack, turn to section 107.

— 88 —

"That's nothing!" Smyth exclaimed in disgust. "Just some fallen trees! Really, Bravo, you're going to have to be more careful!"

"Sorry, sir," Bravo India's platoon leader replied. "You've often said: send it, 'cause you can't mend it."

"True enough," Smyth agreed. "But you could have dispatched a good recon team for a closer look."

"Continue the movement," Bull ordered. Ahead of him the slight hiatus caused by the false report disappeared, and the skimmers flitted once more toward the forest. Bromley altered his vision block to display thermal images and found that even then he couldn't spot his moving infantry. With a satisfied grunt, he turned the display back to normal.

"Alpha India is taking the far way around," Lieutenant Peyton reported. Bull turned his binoculars to the left and caught a glimpse of a skimmer as Peyton's platoon ducked into the far side of the forest.

"On the perimeter," Smyth reported.

"The hill's clear," Bravo India's leader reported.

"Roger," Bull acknowledged. "India, inform me when the forest is secure."

"Wilco."

"Contact! One enemy platoon in the northeast corner of the forest!" Peyton reported hastily. "I've got sights on two squads. Request that India coordinate with my right flank while Bravo stages a cresting maneuver on the hill."

"Cresting maneuver?" Bravo's leader gulped. Since the dawn of long-range weapons, going over the crest of a hill or a mountain has been an invitation for slaughter, presenting a perfect target for even a half-blind enemy. A cresting maneuver required that a platoon act completely inept and wander over the top of a hill, inviting that disaster.

"They're dug in," Peyton explained. "They expect to ambush the road. A cresting on that hill will scare them and catch them unaware. The assault from the two platoons will destroy them."

"What about the tanks?" Bull inquired.

"Ground them," Peyton requested. "The noise would be a dead giveaway."

"Negative," Bull decided. "We'll follow Bravo over the hill. Bravo, move out. This is your chance to excel!" It was a common joke that "a chance to excel" also implied a chance to die horribly.

"Bravo, roger."

Bull nodded to himself as the young platoon leader collected his units and forced them to adopt a sloppy approach to the hill. When they reached the hill, they paused to prepare for the next maneuver.

It was a dangerous ploy. Bravo's leader had his platoon carefully present themselves. Each unit was visible for a moment, bobbing into sight over the hill and then ducking down again, giving an appearance of carelessness, as though the skimmers were just being lazy about their approach. The enemy's response was excellent, hasty fire directed at the last sign of the skimmers. Bravo's platoon suddenly got a bit smarter as the enemy's weapons homed in closer and closer on each skimmer that popped into view. A near miss on Bravo's platoon sergeant caused him to curse, "Fer chrissake! Do it now!"

"Roger," Peyton replied calmly. From behind the hill the

sound of gunfire doubled and trebled. The enemy platoon suddenly found itself in a terribly hot spot.

The enemy has one infantry platoon of four squads, each with an Ordnance value of 2. They are surprised by the sudden attack from the rear and flank and fight using Chart F. The enemy withdraws at the end of three rounds.

The Slammers exploited their position well. Their attack on the unattended enemy flank and rear brings them an excellent advantage, and they attack using Chart A. However, the enemy is not completely powerless. Bull's tanks will not be able to support his infantry in time. All casualties are taken from the skimmers. Only if all skimmer squads are lost will casualties be taken from the hovertanks. Compute Bull's attack strength using only the skimmers.

If the enemy destroys all the Slammers, turn to section 29.

If the enemy withdraws or is destroyed, turn to section 107.

— 89 —

It is impossible to remember how long a second can be. Bull found himself tormented by them as, far ahead of him, unseen and unaided, over thirty skimmers skirted around the forest, hoping not to alarm an alert and ready enemy. Just as Bull had convinced himself that something must have gone wrong, Peyton's voice said, "India, we've grounded. We're going in on foot."

"Roger," Smyth replied, the calm of his voice betraying how tense he was.

"Set," Dyer said softly. Bull wondered why men always whispered over the comm. when they were supporting an ambush.

Bull stole a look at his battle map and nearly jumped out of his skin when he failed to detect the lights of Alpha India's troopers.

With a burst of relief close to pain, he remembered that there wouldn't be any telltales on the display, since the

Slammers didn't have their usual tracking satellites to keep tabs on them. The marking beacon was as much line of sight now as their communications.

"Bravo, commence exercise," Peyton said finally.

Bull glanced up to the hill and the skimmers in front of him as Bravo India's platoon leader replied, "Roger, on the way."

The little skimmers charged gamely up the hill, cresting it and presenting a perfect target to the startled enemy, who had been expecting the Slammers to march up the road and into their guns. The enemy responded well enough as Bravo India poured over the hill and headed for what seemed certain massacre.

Then Alpha India opened fire. Instantly, the pitch of the enemy's gunplay dipped in shock at being fired upon almost from their rear. It picked up again but was not nearly as intense as their opening salvo.

"Move out!" Bull roared as soon as he deemed the crescendo of gunfire loud enough to cover the sound of his hovertanks. "Gun 'em!"

In response, the huge blowers roared into full speed, gathering momentum to crest the steep hill ahead. Bull reveled at the sight of two platoons of tanks charging in the bright sun. The enemy was certainly doomed.

A roar of deeper gunfire startled Bull from his pleasant thought.

"Enemy tank platoon in the forest northwest!" Bravo's leader reported anxiously. "They've just fired on Alpha India!"

"Continue the assault!" Bull replied. "Tango and Alpha Tango, retarget to the woods northwest! Full barrage!"

"Ready!" Dyer replied instantly.

"Fire!" The air quivered as it was sundered by a volley of thunderbolts which rained from the hill into the forest. The first volley tore the trees into pulp, revealing the poorly camouflaged enemy tanks to the sights of Bull's tanks. "Get 'em again!"

The enemy has one platoon of infantry in the forest. Four tanks are hidden in the forest to the north of the hill and northwest of the forest where the infantry are hiding. The infantry platoon has four squads, each with an Ordnance value of 1. The tanks each have an Ordnance value of 2. The enemy attacks using Chart E and withdraws after three rounds of combat.

The Slammers are not perfectly arrayed for this larger battle. They attack using Chart C.

If the enemy destroys Combat Group Foxtrot, turn to section 29.

If the enemy is destroyed or withdraws, record your losses and turn to section 108.

— 90 —

"Via!" someone yelled. A rattle of tribarrels tightened Bull's heart. "They got flankers! We're hit!"

"Bravo, attack!" Peyton yelled in desperation. "They found us!"

Ahead of him Bull saw Bravo India bravely charge over the hill. The situation was wrong, but under control. Bravo India would do to the enemy infantry what Alpha India had planned to do.

Then white hell licked the hilltop as four bolts of energy played across the plains from the woods to the north. Instantly Bravo India disintegrated from a fighting platoon into a mass of dead or dazed men huddling in despair.

"Tango, traverse! Fire on the woods!" Bull roared. His tanks' barrels swiveled toward the woods and unleashed death, matched a moment later by the roar of Dyer's tanks.

"India is committed," Smyth said tightly.

The enemy has a platoon of tanks in the woods north of the hill and northwest of the forest. The four tanks have an Ordnance value of 2 each. The four squads of enemy infantry in the forest have an Ordnance value of 1 each. The enemy attacks using Chart D.

The Slammers attack using Chart C.

If the enemy destroys the Slammers, turn to section 29.

If the Slammers defeat the enemy or the enemy withdraws, turn to section 108.

— 91 —

"That's infantry, all right!" Pete Smyth agreed.

"And there are tanks on the hill northwest, just to the right of the road as it enters the forest," Lieutenant Dyer added.

"Looks like we've found an ambush," Peyton noted.

"Okay," Bull told them, "here's what we do. Bravo India, swing south around the flank of the platoon you found. India will assault it and you'll attack its flank when it engages India."

"Roger."

"Alpha India, swing right to the east around your hill and be ready to head to the east side of the forest that infantry platoon you spotted is in. Alpha Tango, engage that infantry platoon, moving toward it and aid Alpha India in the attack."

"Roger."

"My platoon will take out the tanks on the hill," Bull finished. "Any comments?"

"Negative." "Go for it!" "Ready to move," the others responded.

"Move out," Bull ordered.

Bravo India was the first platoon to move, flitting carefully to the south side of the road and toward the blind side of the enemy platoon. Alpha India began its maneuver to slip to the east side of its hill at nearly the same time, while Alpha Tango edged closer to the hill to get a better aim on its target.

"Lariat Two Six, prepare to engage tanks on the hill to the northwest," Bull told his platoon.

"Got 'em!" Lewis replied. "I'll take the one to the right."

"The one in the middle," Sergeant Healey added.

"I'd take them all, only it wouldn't be fair," Sergeant Gleeson quipped, "so I'll take the one to the left."

"Very well, mark your targets well," Bull said. "I want first-round kills."

"India, this is Bravo India. Set. Over."

"Roger, moving," Smyth replied. Bull glanced to his left to watch Lieutenant Smyth's platoon move out west down the road toward the enemy infantry platoon. It was tough going into a known ambush.

"Alpha India, set," Peyton informed him.

"Alpha Tango, set," Dyer added.

"On my command," Bull replied, and the acknowledgments came back in unison.

Bull kept his eyes on Smyth's platoon. The minute the enemy engaged, Bull wanted the rest of his command to open fire. That way there would be no chance for the enemy to regroup or move about. Slowly the lead elements crept toward the reported enemy position. Bull watched the telltale lights of the infantry skimmers on his computer display. Three hundred, two hundred, one hundred meters!

A slight pop came to his ears.

"Now!" Bull roared. "Foxtrot, attack!"

The air shook as two tank platoons and two infantry platoons simultaneously opened fire. Ahead of him Bull could see at least one of the enemy's tanks blow up, showering the air with hot metal and dead men. To his left Alpha Tango was tearing the woods down around the enemy infantry while Alpha India blazed across the open plain to occupy the eastern edge of the forest. But it was not all easy. Pete Smyth's India had taken a full barrage of fire in that first exchange, and many of his skimmers smoldered in the afternoon sun, their riders missing or dead. Then, just as Peyton's platoon neared the forest, a barrage of blue-green powergun bolts flamed across the valley from the forest due west, betraying in a deadly manner the existence of a third and unknown enemy infantry platoon.

The enemy has three infantry platoons and one tank platoon. All platoons are at full strength of four units each. Each infantry squad has an Ordnance value of 1, and each tank has an Ordnance value of 2. The enemy attacks using Chart D and withdraws after three rounds.

The Slammers attack using Chart B.

If the enemy destroys the Slammers, turn to section 29.

If the enemy is destroyed or withdraws, turn to section 109.

— 92 —

"There's nothing there!" Timmons cried. "No infantry, at least."

Bull examined the image closely before deciding that he agreed with his driver. Bravo India's leader was known to be skittish; this was just an example. To be fair, he switched to infrared but could find no sign of an enemy.

"I don't see it," Bull told the young platoon leader bluntly. "I think you're mistaken. Keep moving, but be cautious."

"Roger," Bravo's leader replied meekly.

The three infantry platoons turned northward, following the road. Peyton's platoon started to cross the open plain to the forest to the north while Bravo India nosed about the mountain to the west and Smyth's India platoon prepared a cautious recon of the open plains northward. With the area cleared, Bull's two tank platoons rounded the bend and headed north, preparing to follow the road as it snaked its way west and through the woods at the base of the mountain. The last tank had just turned when the unmistakable sound of a buzzbomb coming from a long way off startled them.

Normally, a buzzbomb fired from a distance didn't stand a chance against a Slammer tank. It would be destroyed by the all-powerful Hammer howitzers. But the all-powerful Hammer howitzers were with the rest of the regiment—on their way to another war on another planet circling another star.

"Dodge!" Bull roared. "All units dodge!"

The command saved someone's life. The buzzbomb snaked between two tanks and buried itself in the ground beyond. But more buzzbombs took its place. There *was* an enemy infantry platoon in the woods!

"Return fire!" Bull ordered his tanks. Just as the first salvo roared across the valley, four enemy tanks opened fire on Bull's infantry from the hill to the northwest. "Alpha Tango, engage!"

Then buzzbombs appeared everywhere.

"We've got a platoon north!"

"A platoon west!"

"We're surrounded!"

The enemy has three infantry platoons of four squads each (Ordnance value 1 per squad) and one tank platoon of four tanks (Ordnance value 2 per tank). The enemy attacks using Chart B and withdraws after three rounds of combat.

The Slammers fight using Chart D.

If the Slammers are destroyed, turn to section 29.

If the enemy withdraws or is defeated, turn to section 109.

— 93 —

The battle raged on, but behind the roar of the powerguns and the flare of energy bolts licking across the plain were men. Jebbitt's men were tired. They'd been on the run for months and were making one more stand in a series of countless such stands. Bull Bromley's Slammers were a mixture of fresh, battle-ready men and wise, combat-trained fighters. Bull's commanders knew that the enemy was playing for top stakes—not just the equipment in the wreck, but the whole of Hammer's regiment. When it came down to it, the difference in the men decided the battle.

Men like Sergeant Gleeson, who, when his main gun jammed, flattened the enemy with the weight of his tank, daring the buzzbombs. And Sergeant Biddle, who lead his squad into a frontal assault on the heaviest enemy position. Biddle's squad paid the price and got the victory. The enemy infantry broke when Biddle's squad demolished the two squads facing it. Gleeson's charges finished the job.

The remnants of the enemy infantry fled.

"Regroup, move out," Bull ordered, leaving no time for his men to think, to worry. The tanks swept by the town— Sergeant Gleeson had cleared it well enough—and through the next town, phaseline Copper. Beyond that the road swung to the west toward their goal, then back to the north, passing through a small forest at the end of the valley, with a mountain on the right and a hill to the west.

Bull worried about that forest and decided that the best way to allay his fears was to fire probing shots at it. His first shot went into the trees on the left of the road, his second to the right. He had just about decided that his fears were groundless when two bolts fired back at him.

"Via!" Timmons swore, swerving the great hovertank too late.

The enemy have four hovertanks in the woods. Each tank has an Ordnance value of 4. They attack using Chart D and withdraw after three rounds of combat.

The Slammers attack using Chart B.

If the Slammers are destroyed, turn to section 29.

If the enemy is defeated or withdraws, turn to section 67.

— 94 —

"Must be getting old," Lewis muttered to himself. "There's nothing but peaceful villagers in that town."

"Gulf Niner Zero, set," Lewis told Bromley, indicating that his section was in position to cover Bull's bound.

"Moving," Bull responded. Behind him, his tank section roared toward the town. They had just entered it when a whoosh erupted. Lewis could see the contrails of two buzzbombs as they headed unerringly for Bull's tank.

The enemy has a platoon of skimmer-mounted infantry in the town. Each of the four squads has an Ordnance value of 2. The enemy has surprised the Slammers and attacks using Chart B. The enemy withdraws after three rounds of combat because of ammunition shortages.

The Slammers are surprised. They attack using Chart D.

If the Slammers are destroyed, turn to section 29.

If the enemy withdraws or is defeated, turn to section 93.

— 95 —

Since when did humble villagers wear army boots? Lewis asked himself.

"Better have a look at this while I set the coordinates," Sam Lewis radioed to Lieutenant Bromley, sending the display on a different channel. As Bull examined his screen, Lewis quickly got the coordinates for the points of fire. He didn't want to hurt the village or the people, and there was a good chance that the Slammers could fire surgically—well, better than usual.

"Yep. They look great until you see their boots and the weapons slung on their shoulders," Bull agreed.

"One's got a buzzbomb in his truck," Ennis added.

"The coordinates are set," Lewis told them. "Request coordinated fire on my control."

"You've got it. Wait," Bull confirmed. On another channel Bull called Dyer and told him to slave his guns to Lewis's control while Engles relayed the same information to the rest of the platoon. "Fire under your control," Bull finally told Lewis.

"Roger. Firing now," Lewis replied, depressing the trigger on his main gun. Simultaneously two platoons roared out and licked the edge of the town with white hell.

The enemy has a skimmer-mounted platoon of infantry in the village. The platoon has four squads, each with an Ordnance value of 2. They fight using Chart D.

The Slammers, firing with accuracy almost as great as computer-controlled fire, can surgically assault the enemy. They attack using Chart A. The Slammers' infantry Ordnance is NOT counted in this attack (count the Ordnance of their tanks only).

If the Slammers are destroyed, turn to section 29.

If the enemy is destroyed or retreats, turn to section 93.

— 96 —

Fire from the tanks caught Group Foxtrot in the front while fire from the village caught the combat group in the right flank. It was devastating. Skimmers were obliterated, and Bull's tanks rode in a storm of cyan death, battered and tossed about as their driver desperately tried to stave off disaster. For some it worked, for others it did not.

Bull's command worked its way forward under the blistering fire and finally approached the edge of the first town. As if on a signal, fire from the enemy withered and died out. Maybe they had reach their ammunition allocation or been scared by the rigid determination of the Slammers. Or maybe, in the rubble of town and forest, all the enemy had been obliterated. Bull couldn't tell.

"Hot work!" Timmons commented brusquely.

"Good driving," Ennis complimented him.

"Hey! I've got places to go, things to do," Timmons explained, "and a women to see." Sara Engles snorted.

"Silence," Bull chided his crew gently. "Mike, this is Two Zero, report."

"This is Juliet Niner Zero, operational," Smyth replied instead of his usual, "Ready to move."

"Roger," Bull acknowledged. "Bravo Two Victor Niner Zero, Mike Two Zero."

"Victor Niner Zero," the sergeant major replied.

"Receive the casualties," Bull ordered.

"It'll be our honor."

"November Fower Mike, this is Mike Two Zero. Transfer casualties to Victor Niner Zero. We move in two. Over," Bull ordered.

Two minutes later the skimmers moved out, some with two men doubled up and others barely holding together, but they moved. Showing no fear, they secured phaseline Copper in a short time, pronouncing it clear for the hovertanks and the softskinned vehicles. Moving out of the city, the road turned west toward their destination, then made a sharp right turn north to skirt around the mountain and pass through a small forest.

Turn to section 82.

— 97 —

"Switch frequencies, we've been compromised!" Bull exclaimed.

"Frequencies switched," Sara Engles responded in a tone that told Bull he was too late. "Your callsign is November Fower Mike Two Zero at regiment level, Whiskey Tree Yankee—"

"I've got it!" Bull cut her off. "November Fower Mike, this is Mike Two Zero, join the net." He was flouting all the standards by saying that, but he had no time.

"Alpha Six Juliet," Smyth replied.

"Get your pongoes around either flank and engage those bastards!" Bull ordered.

"Done."

"Company!" Bull barked to Sara.

"This is Kilo Six November; am engaging closer," the voice of lieutenant Dyer said instantly.

"Good going!" Bull agreed. To Sara he asked, "Did we lose them?" meaning the enemy. Because the enemy had salvaged Slammer skimmers from the transport wreck, they had access to all the standard communications frequencies and callsigns used by Hammer's regiment. The CEOIs that Bull had issued to his men were special issue—the enemy didn't have them.

Enemy! Bull thought to himself. Jebbitt, mostly likely! Ha! I've beaten you before! This is just the afterbirth.

The enemy has two platoons of skimmer-mounted infantry, with four squads each. Each squad has an Ordnance value of 2. The enemy attacks using Chart D and withdraws after three rounds.

The Slammers attack using Chart C.

If the enemy destroys the Slammers, turn to section 29.

If the Slammers destroy the enemy, or the enemy withdraws, turn to section 105.

— 98 —

"Bluejay Five!" Engles exclaimed. "That's the codeword that our communications have been compromised!"

"They're using some of our skimmers," Bull said by way of agreement. "Switch to the emergency frequencies in the CEOI. Let me know what my callsign is."

"Roger," Engles replied. As she switched, Bull had time to ponder the implications of this news. The enemy had copies of the emergency issue CEOIs on the skimmers they had no doubt stolen from the crashed transport. They could read them, switch to Bull's frequencies, and still compromise his communications, but it would be harder. The bigger problem was that his own men weren't trained to use CEOIs. Another problem was those skimmers.

"Your callsign is—" Sara began.

"November Fower Mike Two Zero, this is Alpha Six Juliet. Over," Pete Smyth's voice interrupted.

"Go ahead," Bull replied.

"Engaging two infantry platoons in two forests. Request assistance." Pete Smyth's voice was calm, but Bull could tell the lieutenant was strained.

"On the way," Bull replied, glancing at the callsigns now listed in front of him. "Kilo Six November Niner Zero, this is Mike Two Zero. Engage the enemy."

"Roger," Dyer replied.

The enemy has two platoons of skimmer-mounted infantry, each of four squads. Each squad has an Ordnance value of 2. They have surprised the Slammers, who are now working under the disadvantage of difficult communications. The enemy attacks using Chart C and withdraws after three rounds of combat.

The Slammers attack using Chart D.

If the Slammers are destroyed, turn to section 29.

If the enemy withdraws or is destroyed, turn to section 105.

— 99 —

"Bluejay Five?" Ennis said, puzzled.

"Switching frequencies," Engles told Bull quietly. To Ennis she added in a lofty tone, "To emergency communications frequencies. That's the codeword meaning we've been compromised."

"The enemy has some of our skimmers," Bull explained.

"Where'd they get them?" Timmons queried.

"November Fower Mike Two Zero, this is Alpha Six Juliet Niner Zero. Am engaging the enemy," the voice of Pete Smyth informed him.

"Roger." Bull stole an inquiring look at Sara.

"Bravo India is now Kilo Fower Charlie Niner Zero," Sara supplied.

"Kilo Fower Charlie, this is Mike Two Zero. Engage enemy to the east," Bull ordered. Silence greeted him. Damn! He'd have to call Dyer and tell him to get that section up to the battle.

Look at the Communications Equipment Operating Instructions section appendix of this book.

If you think that Lieutenant Dyer's callsign is K6N90Y or K6N24Y, turn to section 112.

If you think that Lieutenant Dyer's callsign is Z8G36A or A2A14Y, turn to section 113.

If you can't make up your mind, turn to section 114.

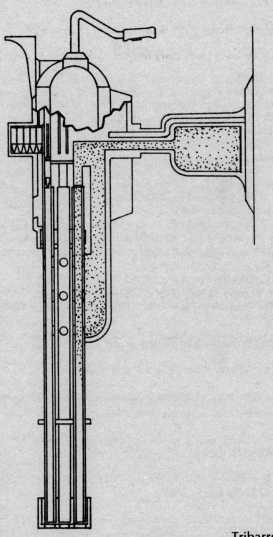

Tribarrel

— 100 —

"Switching frequencies!" Sara said calmly. "You are now November Four Mike Two Zero." Bull's right vision block cleared to display the list of the new callsigns for his units. Ennis pursed his lips as he studied the new callsigns, just in case he had to help out.

"November Four Mike, this is Mike Two Zero," Bull said.

"November Four Mike Two Zero, this is Alpha Six Juliet Niner Zero," Pete Smyth's voice replied.

"This is Mike Two Zero, sitrep," Bull responded, asking for the situation report.

"Have engaged two enemy platoons equipped with skimmers. Have evaded all radio misdirection. Are pressing the attack," Pete Smyth replied formally, adding: "No problem!"

The enemy has two skimmer-mounted platoons with four squads each. Each squad has an Ordnance value of 2. The enemy attacks using Chart D and withdraws after three rounds of fighting.

The Slammers attack using Chart B.

If the Slammers are defeated, turn to section 29.

If the enemy is destroyed or withdraws, turn to section 106.

— 101 —

"Roger," Bull acknowledged. The enemy had Slammer skimmers with Slammer radios; the enemy could hear them. "Foxtrot, this is Six. Bluejay Five." To his comm. chief he said, "Switch to the CEOI frequencies, Sara."

"Switched," Engles replied. Bull glanced at his CEOI, looking for Sam Lewis's callsign.

If you believe that Bull Bromley should use Z8G14Y as Sergeant Lewis's callsign, turn to section 115.

If you believe that Bull should use Z8G24Y as Sergeant Lewis's callsign, turn to section 116.

— 102 —

"Switching to emergency frequencies," Engles replied calmly. "Your callsign is November Fower Mike Two Zero."

"Roger." Bull pulled out the emergency CEOI codebook and wished that the enemy's stolen skimmers didn't have them as well. Might as well wish for artillery!

"Zulu Ate Golf Tree Six, this is Golf Niner Zero. Engage westward," Bull said to Sergeant Gleeson. "Timmons, get this bucket where it has to go!" he added to his driver. As the tank turned to head toward the western forest, Bull looked for Sam Lewis's tank but couldn't see it in the barrage of powerbolts. Ahead of him it looked like rays of lightning were striking from the forest at all angles.

"Golf One Fower, this is Golf Niner Zero," Bull called to Lewis.

"One Fower, we're alive," Lewis said tightly. The tone of his voice told Bull that Sam didn't have time to be sociable.

Bull looked around for the infantry platoon that had been following him and could see nothing of it.

He groped for the callsign in his CEOI. "Kilo Fower Charlie this is Mike Two Zero. Engage to the west."

"This is Kilo Fower Charlie, roger," Bravo's platoon leader replied. Instantly, the area was swarming with skimmers that flitted north then west to attack the enemy in the forest due west.

"Kilo Six November Nine Zero, this is Mike Two Zero. Report," Bull called to Dyer.

"It's in the bag!" Dyer replied. Indeed it was, Bull agreed, glancing east behind him to see the withering fire Dyer's tanks had laid on the enemy. The forest that had hidden the enemy was now a bare plain littered with pulped remnants of its trees. Peyton's infantry was advancing to assault the scattered enemy. Just as Bull decided that the situation to the east was under control, a flock of buzzbombs raced toward Dyer's tanks.

The enemy has two infantry platoons mounted on Hammer's regiment skimmers. Each platoon has four squads, each with an Ordnance value of 2. The enemy attacks using Chart D and withdraws after three rounds.

The Slammers attack using Chart C.

If the enemy destroys the Slammers, turn to section 29.

If the enemy withdraws or is destroyed, turn to section 117.

— **103** —

Bull thought furiously. Skimmers in the woods! No one on Maffren had skimmers, not even Jebbitt's Raiders. They had come against the Slammers using tracked vehicles only. The one place the enemy could get skimmers was from the wrecked transport. It was too much of a coincidence to believe that the enemy would be close enough to the wreck to salvage the skimmers, unless that enemy had sabotaged the *Vindictive* and knew exactly where it would come down. The Maffrens didn't have either the technology or the guts for such an operation. It had to be Jebbitt.

Those thoughts spawned others. Jebbitt now had skimmers. He probably had hovertanks, too, but those hadn't got this far south yet. They would have no trouble finding the frequencies the Slammers used for combat. Bull's command was using the training frequency, but even so, it was only a matter of time until their communications were intercepted.

Bull swore. They would have to switch frequencies. Of course! "Bluejay Five" was the codeword that communications were compromised and the order to use the CEOIs.

"Switch to emergency CEOI," Bull said to Engles.

"Switched," she replied. "You're November Four Mike Two Zero."

"Put the callsigns on number four," Bull ordered. He had four display screens around him. On the fourth appeared the complete useful list of callsigns for his command and the rest of the Slammers.

"Mike Two Zero, this is Juliet Niner Zero," Pete Smyth called.

"How does it look?" Bull asked.

"Rough. Can you support?"

Bull could see ahead that the three infantry platoons were taking a pasting from the enemy fire. "Roger. By sections."

"Thanks."

"Whiskey Tree Yankee this is Yankee Niner Zero. Assault by sections."

"November Niner Zero, on the way!" Dyer replied swiftly. Out of the corner of his eye Bull could see Dyer's tank. The bright flame of a powerbolt flowered from it and tore the forest down around the infantry in the woods.

Sergeant Lewis's section was also firing, but on the woods to the west, while Brad's section maneuvered closer to the forest. It was going to be just a little bit sticky, Bull decided.

The enemy has two platoons of skimmer-mounted infantry in the forests to the east and west of the road. Each platoon has four squads with an Ordnance value of 2 each. The enemy attacks using Chart B and withdraws after three rounds of combat.

The Slammers attack using Chart C.

If the enemy destroys the Slammers, turn to section 29.

If the enemy withdraws or is destroyed, turn to section 118.

— 104 —

It had to be their own skimmers, salvaged from the wreck, Bull thought. That meant the enemy knew their combat frequencies. Bull swore. Engles switched to the CEOI frequencies while Bull pondered the implications. At least he had decided to order the special CEOIs instead of relying on the standard-issue CEOI books found aboard every Slammer vehicle, including the stolen skimmers.

"Get me Smyth," Bull told Engles.

". . . Two Zero, this is Juliet Niner Zero. Request support by sections," Smyth was saying.

"This is Mike Two Zero," Engles prompted Bull, who glared at her and said, "wilco." He tapped up the CEOI on his number four display.

"November Niner Zero, Mike Two Zero. Assist to east. Support by sections," he told Lieutenant Dyer.

"Wilco."

"Golf One Fower, we support by section. You have the hot seat," Bull told Sam Lewis.

"On the way," Lewis replied steadily. To his left Bull watched the two tanks of Lewis's section charge toward the enemy while Bull's pair of tanks began to lay down a barrage on the forest to the west of the road. Taking a moment to glance at his beleaguered infantry, he cursed himself for not putting his tanks out first. This sort of treatment would hardly heat their iridium armor. Instead, skimmers were being dyed blood red.

The enemy has two platoons of skimmer-mounted infantry, one east and one west of the road. Each platoon has four squads, each with an Ordnance value of 2. The enemy attacks using Chart C and withdraws after three rounds of combat.

The Slammers, battered but quickly recovering from their shock, attack well using Chart B.

If the enemy destroys the Slammers, turn to section 29.

If the Slammers destroy the enemy or the enemy withdraws, turn to section 118.

— 105 —

The enemy skimmers may have started the battle, but Bull's panzers finished it. Barrage after barrage of heavy tank guns tore through the two forests. Bull noticed one powerbolt flick a skimmer against a tree and shatter both tree and skimmer. Another powerbolt disintegrated one tree and set a second on fire. In short order the two forests had become nothing but stubble, bent metal, and dead men.

"Cease fire!" Bull roared. "There's nothing left to hit."

As the air cleared and the filth of battle drifted away, Bull could see that his infantry hadn't been completely saved by his armor's firepower. In plain view were the smudges that marked the remains of skimmers and riders.

"Juliet Niner Zero, this is Mike Two Zero," Bull called.

"This is Juliet Niner Zero. It's bad," Lieutenant Smyth informed him. "Some of the squads got hit hard."

"Got a couple of wounded men here," Lieutenant Peyton added in a defiant tone, "and a bunch of brave dead men."

"Get the wounded back to the . . ." Bull paused, considering what callsign Sergeant Major Ogren should use.

"Bravo Two Victor Niner Zero," the sergeant major called, answering Bull's question. It seemed he considered his softskinned charges to be the third tank platoon. "Ready to receive wounded. Over," Ogren stated.

"Roger." To Engles he added, "Relay that." Sara nodded calmly. Bull watched with clenched fists as his battered combat group slowly reformed, the skimmers ferrying their wounded to the softskinned vehicles in the rear before returning to the formation.

Finally they moved on.

Mark your casualties on the chart and turn to section 119.

— 106 —

The two infantry platoons nearest the forest made heavy use of the tank sections attached to them while the third platoon under the direction of Lieutenant Dyer, moved swiftly and quietly until it was on the road heading north. Then it split, one section of infantry and one tank attacking west, the other group attacking east.

The sudden onslaught from another quarter proved too much for the Raiders. Those that could, ran. Those that couldn't, died. In the end, neither forest stood. Littered among the dead trees were dead ambushers.

"November Four Mike, this is Mike Two Zero. Regroup," Bull radioed his command.

"Whew doggy! Did we ever show 'em!" an unidentified voice cheered.

"Send your casualties back to Bravo Two Victor Niner Zero," Bull ordered. B2V90 was the callsign for the third tank platoon. In a fit of humor no one knew he possessed, Sergeant Major Ogren had taken this callsign for his group of softskinned vehicles.

"Roger," Smyth replied. "Alpha Six Juliet, ready to move."

"Kilo Six November, ready," Dyer added.

"Alpha Two Alpha, ready," Peyton finished.

"Victor?" Bull asked the sergeant major.

"Get out of the way; we're chargin'!" Ogren replied.

"November Four Mike, continue march," Bull called.

Dyer's section and Bravo India platoon returned to the left flank while Pete Smyth's reinforced platoon surged to the front of the wedge. Peyton's Alpha India platoon with Sergeant Lewis's tank section quickly got into position on the right. It was Smyth's game now.

Turn to section 120.

— 107 —

The air crackled with the heat of powerbolts as they tore through the forest. The skimmers caught the brunt of it, and many of them flashed through incandescence into ash. Others were not so lucky as powerbolts tore through the innards of men and left them brief seconds of shocked horror before they died.

Often the only difference between the victor and the vanquished is that one can smell death and the other smells of death. That was the way of it now. A stunned silence fell. From somewhere a light wind blew, tearing through the curtain of smoke that was part metal, part man, and mostly forest, to reveal the minor hell that had been created here.

Bull clutched the breech of his powergun for support. Here and there a tree in that forest still stood, but most were either shredded or lying at some weird angle as the very ground beside them had been vaporized. He couldn't see any of the enemy dead. Maybe they'd suffered fewer casualties; more likely their casualties had been more totally obliterated than Foxtrot's.

Foxtrot's casualties were grim. Those who weren't dead suffered from a plethora of shrapnel wounds, violently amputated limbs, missing eyes, and sucking chest wounds.

"Get the medics up here!" Bull shouted over the laserlink "On the double!"

"Your shouting won't help the living nor raise the dead," Sergeant Major Ogren shot back hotly.

"Get up here!" Bull roared back. "All Indias, prepare to hand over wounded."

In scant moments the remains of the three infantry platoons were formed up again, ready to press on. Bull could hardly believe it.

"India, this is Foxtrot. Contact me when you're ready to move," Bull said to Pete Smyth, knowing that the others were listening.

"India, ready."

"Alpha India, ready now." Peyton's voice was shaky.

"Bravo India, ready to move."

"Roger," Bull replied with deep feeling. "Thank you," he added after a moment. "Foxtrot this is Six. Move out!" Bull ordered.

The three infantry platoons headed north, arrayed on either side of the road, with the two tank platoons nudging them gently from the rear. The softskinneds were slower in getting started, having to detach a small section to take care of those wounded who could survive if they received immediate medical attention.

It was hard for Bull to comprehend that some men who had survived the battle would not survive the day. "Triage" was a medical term long familiar to Bull from his younger days. It meant that those who would survive if aided immediately would be treated first. Those who could wait for attention would be treated next, and those whom no treatment could save would be given drugs to make them comfortable while they died.

The road turned right, and Bull let his thoughts stray with it. Ahead of them was a forest on the right and wide fields on the left. Almost due north was phaseline Amber.

Bull studied the woods carefully. He didn't like them. He had just decided that it was worth the risk of lobbing in a couple of scare shots when four well-aimed bolts of light struck out from the woods themselves.

"Skimmers, attack by pincer; blowers, return fire!" Bull roared, as Ennis fired the huge powergun on their tank. "Good shooting," Bull said to his corporal.

"Ha! Got you now, Foxtrot! Eat this!" A voice sneered over the radio.

"Bluejay Five! Bluejay Five! The bird has squawked!" Another voice radioed imploringly.

If you have "Bluejay Five" written down on a piece of paper, turn to section 123.

Otherwise, turn to section 124.

— 108 —

Bull's panzers destroyed the tanks in the forest, and the skimmers took care of the infantry in the woods. It was that easy. At least that's how it would appear in Bull's report. But the report wouldn't record the sounds of powerbolts tearing through the air, or of men's dying screams, or of the forest groaning as it collapsed. The report would include the numbers of wounded and dead, but it would not record how long Bull had known each man or whose name a dying corporal had cried with his last breath. Nor would the report say anything about that horrifying moment when the only question on a soldier's mind is: Am I still alive?

For one brief moment, all was quiet, then men finished their dying or started their screaming, and hell took one step away from the earth—not a very distant step, just a hop. Death would come again this day.

"Report," Bull forced himself to say.

"Alpha India, ready," Peyton replied, once again the calm, taciturn leader.

"India, we've got wounded," Smyth reported.

"Bravo India, request aid for the wounded," Bravo's platoon leader responded.

"Sierra Mike—" Bull began.

"We're on the way," Sergeant Major Ogren cut in. "Have the wounded ready for loading; we haven't got all day."

As Bull tried to think of something to say in reply, he absently noticed a streak of armor on his tank that still glowed red hot from a glancing blow. So close to being dead and I hadn't noticed it till now, Bull mused.

"Roger," he finally managed to say. "Foxtrot, move in two."

Two minutes later India moved forward flanked by Alpha India and Bravo India. Bull's panzers waited impatiently until the infantry advance had gone far enough.

"Tangos, move," Bull ordered. The move forward was quiet, with no incidents. The panzers soon came abreast of the torn forest where the enemy tanks had been destroyed.

Bull wasn't sure how many gutted tanks he spotted in the forest—there were too many pieces.

The two flanking infantry platoons flitted wide about the phaseline while Pete Smyth's India platoon took quick, cautious darts toward the town. All was quiet.

Time beat on Bull Bromley's mind. Each second might mean another Slammer dead, another lost chance, another enemy unit blocking their way.

"Report," he said suddenly, deciding to force Smyth to speed it up. The infantry were doubtless edgy, but Bull couldn't afford to be overcautious. A skimmer flitted into view as though in reply to his order.

"Nothing so far," Smyth replied, his tone implying that things might suddenly change.

"Roger," Bull acknowledged. "Foxtrot, secure Amber," he ordered. Timmons gunned the tank in response, and they galloped toward the distant town. As they neared it and could make out the faces of cheerful townspeople waving at them, Bull was convinced that he had made the right decision and saved vital time.

"Contact!" Smyth cried. "Contact, sheer off! Enemy in the town—they're holding the villagers hostage!"

Two buzzbombs roared straight at Bull's tank from close range. "Eat that, Foxtrot!" a voice jeered over the radio.

"Bluejay Five! Bluejay Five! The bird has squawked!" Lieutenant Dyer roared over the radio. In front of him the village erupted in a flare of white light, arcing through the compass to strike at skimmer and hovertank alike. Timmons vainly tried to dodge the two oncoming buzzbombs while Ennis hosed them with his sidearm. Bull hastily aimed his weapon and started firing at the front of the contrail, but he knew he hadn't a chance.

If you have "Bluejay Five" written on your piece of paper, turn to section 126.

If you do not, turn to section 127.

— 109 —

The world was a barrage of deathly light, and Group Foxtrot was in the center of it all. From all around them powerbolts large and small poured in while they returned their white death with equal abandon. Individual scenes remained in Bull's memory for many years afterward, but the whole battle was lost in a maze of similar battles, similar scares, and similar thrills. He remembered distinctly one of his pongoes racing across the fields, dismounted but unafraid, dodging bolt after bolt until he was right among the enemy platoon. The platoon broke and fled from that one brave man, but not before a burst of brilliant, blue-green light hit the trooper and turned him into a blazing torch for one indelible instant.

Bull also remembered screaming in panic as a buzzbomb zeroed right in on his tank—and hit! Timmons had swerved the tank just in time to deflect the missile, leaving a white-hot score on the tank's iridium armor. Bull remembered glancing at his trembling hands and realizing that everyone else in the tank was trembling as the armored vehicle shook on its cushion of air.

Bull forgot the fierceness with which he emptied his turret gun into the offending bit of forest, bringing the tank's main gun to bear only when his own weapon was too hot to handle. Suddenly there were no more enemy in that forest, so he changed back to bombard the smoldering hulks of the enemy tanks. Soon they, too, were reduced to useless scrap, so he charged west to the final enemy position in the woods. And then it was over. The enemy had fled or been crushed by the fierce onslaught of avenging Slammers.

Bull pulled himself together. "Cease fire!" he called, but there was silence already. Looking about, he could see Sam Lewis, his platoon sergeant, wave to him from a distant tank. Lewis's tank had also taken a hit. A chunk of armor was missing from its front, but it was still a serviceable vessel of war.

"Report," Bull ordered in a more collected tone. Slowly he could make out the carnage and wreckage that didn't distinguish between the enemy and his own troops. The butcher's bill was high, but there was still fight left in his men.

"Sierra Mike, we're ready for casualties," the sergeant major reported first.

"Roger," Bull acknowledged. "Foxtrot, send your casualties to Sierra Mike."

"This is India, roger," Pete Smyth responded. Then, just as Bull had hoped, "Ready to move."

"Alpha India, ready to move."

"Bravo India, ready to move."

"Tango Alpha, ready to move."

They were badly battered, his men, but they weren't beaten. For a moment Bull couldn't say anything. He just let his eyes scan the stained fields littered with blood and bodies. Then he pulled himself together. There were other Slammers still alive, who would be dead if they got to the wreck too late.

"Move out, full speed," Bull ordered.

"On the way!" Smyth replied cheerfully. Ahead of him Bull watched the remaining skimmers of India flit off through the forest, flanked by the skimmers of Alpha India and Bravo India. In that instant, seeing those war-scarred skimmers move off like that, Bull knew he wouldn't trade one of them for a regiment.

His tanks followed shortly afterwards, but it was up to the infantry to lead the way through the tight terrain. Bull was counting on the sharp eyes and cautious curiosity of his skimmers to find the enemy before the enemy found them. For all of that, he urged the skimmers to make up for lost time. The infantry responded, pushing their flighty vehicles as hard as possible, riding them like the ancient broncos of Earth's cowboys. They jumped them into ditches, flew them over ridges, and through narrow gorges and defiles.

They made phaseline Brown and cleared it in twelve minutes, a record for movement in a combined arms force. Then they headed south toward the westward turn at phaseline White.

It was Peyton's platoon, heading far off course, that picked up the signal. He recorded it and relayed it back to Bull instantly.

"I caught this on our old combat frequency," Peyton said. The recording went, "—Hyatt. We have secured the fork."

The voice repeated, "D'accord, this is Splinter Hyatt. We have secured the fork, over."

After a moment the voice began again. "D'accord, this is Splinter Hyatt. Over." There was a shorter pause. "Christ! This bloody Slammer gear! Damn this thing! Damn this tank! Switch me to their training freq!"

"They've got hovertanks!" Ennis declared.

"They're going to our frequency," Sara Engles stated.

If you have "Bluejay Five" written on a piece of paper, turn to section 130.

If not, turn to section 129.

— 110 —

Nothing there, Smyth decided. It must have just been my imagination, he chided himself.

"Move on," Smyth ordered his squad. Around him, almost invisible, the rest of his platoon headed up the road.

All the same, something nagged at Smyth, and he kept a careful eye on the two towns as they approached them. That was how he managed to catch sight of the enemy skimmer.

"Enemy platoon in the town, skimmer mounted," he reported instantly. He could see more of them and was sure that he was right and there was a full platoon there.

"Roger. We'll dust 'em up and you can eat 'em," Bull Bromley replied with a drawl. "Send the coordinates."

Deftly, Smyth marked in the coordinates on his battle display and transmitted them to the rest of the combat group. In an instant he was rewarded with the throaty roar of two tank platoons firing in unison on one target. Ahead of him the village disintegrated. From the north a barrage of cyan light replied.

"Bog! Tanks! They got a platoon of tanks in the woods to the north!" Peyton swore roundly.

The enemy has two platoons, one of hovertanks and one of skimmer infantry. Each platoon has four tanks or four squads of infantry. The tanks each have an Ordnance value of 4, while each skimmer squad has an Ordnance value of 2. The enemy attacks using Chart C. They withdraw after three rounds of combat.

The Slammers attack using Chart B.

If the Slammers are destroyed, turn to section 29.

If the Slammers defeat the enemy or drive him off, turn to section 96.

— 111 —

Peyton's command was clearing the end of the woods, and Dyer's command was edging toward the far forest when it happened. Dyer uttered an exclamation that Bull didn't catch, but his binoculars caught Bravo India as it exposed itself heading toward the forest.

The results were instantaneous. Four cyan bolts roared from the forest nearest the platoon and left only vaporized metal where skimmers had been. As if that weren't enough, four more heavy barrels erupted just beside Peyton and tore into Bravo India.

"Yankee, ground and engage!" Bull ordered the tanks. "Juliet, maneuver clear!" It was too late for Bravo India. The remnants of the platoon were engaged in the very difficult job of staying alive.

Just as Bull thought it could get no worse, Smyth's command, which had charged on in the hope of taking Bravo India's assailant in the rear, was blasted by bolts streaming forth from phaseline Gold. Enemy infantry!

The enemy has three platoons: two equipped with four hovertanks each and one platoon of four squads of skimmer-mounted infantry. The skimmer squads have Ordnance values of 2 each while the hovertanks have Ordnance values of 4 each. The enemy attacks using Chart B. They withdraw after three rounds of combat because of a lack of ammunition.

The Slammers attack using Chart C. All casualties must come first from Bravo India, then from other Slammer units.

If the Slammers are destroyed, turn to section 29.

If the Slammers survive, turn to section 36.

— 112 —

"Kilo Six November Niner Zero Yankee, this is Mike Two Zero," Bull called.

"November Niner Zero, go."

"November Niner Zero, contact Kilo Fower Charlie. Get them on the right frequency and move to aid the combat occurring to your east," Bull ordered.

"Roger, on the way."

Bull had to hope that the enemy hadn't caught their change of frequencies. If Bravo India's leader was futilely crying out for orders on a silent net, the enemy might soon become aware of it and draw the only conclusion possible—to turn to the emergency CEOI band. Of course, Bull's combat group was using the training frequency. If the Slammers' equipment salvaged from the wreck by the enemy was tuned to the combat frequency, that gave him a chance.

The roar of gunfire disturbed him. His job was to guard the softskinneds, even while the rest of his command fought an enemy mounted on captured skimmers.

The enemy has two platoons of skimmer-mounted infantry, with four squads each. Each squad has an Ordnance value of 2. The enemy attacks using Chart D and withdraws after three rounds of combat.

The Slammers attack using Chart C.

If the Slammers are destroyed, turn to section 29.

If the Slammers destroy or beat off the enemy, turn to section 106.

— 113 —

"Zulu Ate Golf Tree Six Alpha, this is Mike Two Zero," Bull radioed. He squinted at the CEOI again. Maybe that wasn't quite right.

"This is Golf Tree Six Yankee," the voice of Sergeant Gleeson replied bemusedly.

"Ignore," Engles told him. "You want Kilo Six November Niner Zero Yankee, sir."

Bull blushed.

Turn to section 112.

— 114 —

This is a dead end. A Slammer officer shouldn't be here. Go back to section 99 and make up your mind.

— 115 —

"Zulu Ate Golf One Fower Yankee, this is Golf Niner Zero. Sitrep, over," Bull called over the radio.

"This is Golf One Fower Yankee. Request infantry flanking assault westward," Lewis replied.

"Roger," Bull agreed. "Kilo Fower Charlie Niner Zero, this is Mike Two Zero. Assault west forest."

"Charlie Niner Zero, wilco," Bravo's platoon leader replied. Bull watched as the skimmers of Bravo's platoon passed between his tanks and Lewis's tanks, wheeling first east, then swinging around to the west to assault the enemy infantry on its flank.

"Kilo Six November Niner Zero, this is Mike Two Zero. Sitrep, over."

"This is November Niner Zero. Have ordered Alpha Niner Zero to assist in the assault," Dyer replied tersely.

"Roger." Enemy powerbolts struck at Bull's tank, warming the iridium to a dull red but doing no more damage. Bull looked around and realized that Ennis had been firing steadily at the enemy for several minutes.

The enemy has two platoons with four squads each of skimmer-mounted infantry. Each squad has an Ordnance value of 2. The enemy fights using Chart D and withdraws after three rounds.

The Slammers fight using Chart B.

If the enemy destroys the Slammers, turn to section 29.

If the enemy is destroyed or withdraws, turn to section 117.

— 116 —

"Zulu Ate Golf Two Fower Yankee, this is Golf Niner Zero," Bull called to Lewis. He received no reply. "Are we on the right frequency?" Bull asked his comm. chief, thinking that for once she might not have outguessed him.

"Right frequency, wrong callsign," Engles replied. "Zulu Ate Golf ONE Fower Yankee, this is Golf Niner Zero Alpha."

"Go ahead," Lewis replied.

"I am committing Kilo Fower Charlie to an assault westward in support of us," Bull told his platoon sergeant.

"Roger," Lewis replied. Bull looked around to see that Dyer's platoon was getting active support from Lieutenant Peyton and was giving the enemy a rough go.

"Charlie Niner Zero's on the line," Engles said.

"Charlie Niner Zero, assault west forest," Bull ordered.

"Wilco!"

The enemy has two platoons of skimmer-mounted infantry in the forest. Each platoon has four squads, each with an Ord-

nance value of 2. The enemy attacks using Chart E and withdraws after three rounds of combat.

The Slammers attack using Chart C.

If the enemy destroys the Slammers, turn to section 29.

If the enemy withdraws or is destroyed by the Slammers, turn to section 117.

— 117 —

The enemy, equipped with skimmers and buzzbombs, proved tough to dislodge. They fought well, but they died. Skimmers have two defenses against hovertanks: mobility and dispersion. The enemy had given up his mobility by waiting in the forests, and had compounded the error by not dispersing enough. Bull's infantry exploited their error by deftly deploying and pouring firepower at all the choke points. The end was predetermined.

But not without cost. As the last shots were fired, Bull could see that several of his tanks had received glancing blows; one bore several livid, glowing scars. The infantry had taken it worse. Many of the squads showed signs of depletion. The remaining men looked exhausted, and it was only their second engagement. That was the nature of battle—all adrenaline and no rest.

"I recognize those skimmers," Peyton radioed. "They're ours, all right. I know the platoon they were with. Tough men."

"Where are they now?" Dyer mused.

"November Fower Mike, prepare to move," Bull told them, cutting short the chatter. "Leave the wounded with—" Bull realized he didn't know what Sergeant Major Ogren's callsign should be.

"Mike Two Zero, Bravo Two Victor Niner Zero, ready to receive casualties and prisoners," the sergeant major said with a touch of humor Bull had not known he possessed.

Ogren had taken the callsign for the third tank platoon for his convoy of softskinned vehicles.

"Roger," Bull acknowledged. "November Fower Mike, move in two minutes."

The casualties were hustled back to the softskinneds, and Sergeant Major Ogren detailed a small detachment to deal with the immediate operations. They would catch up long before the line of softskinned vehicles had moved out.

Bull surveyed the terrain ahead. The forest on their left stayed with them for another kilometer. So did the lake to the right of the road, but it went on for another kilometer after that. The road then turned to the northeast and straightened out as it approached the town of Hillstart. Beyond the town was a forest lining the right side of the road all the way to Gold City, phaseline Copper. After Copper the road went west for several kilometers, skirting a mountain on its right side, then turned north to head through a small woods just before the crossroads at phaseline White. At every point there could be an ambush.

"Golf, this is Niner Zero. Move by sections," Bull instructed his platoon, relaying the same instructions to Dyer.

"Yeah," Dyer agreed emphatically. The two platoons split into two sections and the four separate units moved one at a time, sniffing into a new position with each jump and waiting for the next element to move. It was time-consuming, but the leaps and bounds of the hovertanks were fast and far.

Lewis's section was the first to reach the town. Sergeant Lewis was a cautious man who planned to get older. He didn't really like sniffing out towns, especially without an "eye in the sky," the satellite surveillance that the Slammers normally enjoyed. Lewis was expecting something to happen, so he examined the terrain carefully. He was sure that there was nothing wrong, nothing more than curious villagers. Still, he'd always believed in taking a second look.

Look at the picture on the next page.

If you think that Sergeant Lewis should report the town as clear, turn to section 94.

If you think that Sergeant Lewis should report enemy in the town and request that the Slammers fire on a town full of villagers, turn to section 95.

— 118 —

The roar of hovertanks settled the matter. When the two tank platoons engaged each enemy skimmer platoon, the enemy could only die or run. Some died, some ran. Those that cowered in fear were covered by falling trees, trees blasted by the brilliant cyan of pure energy that was a powerbolt. It was not a one-sided fight, however, and Bull's tank bore a glowing white scar where a buzzbomb had nearly finished him. He counted himself lucky, looking at the fallen infantry and smashed skimmers. He didn't have to look long before he remembered why they were there—the wreck's survivors.

Bull was sure now that the enemy knew where the wreck was coming down because they had sabotaged the *Vindictive*. Any Slammers who had survived the crash would desperately need help to fight off Jebbitt's band.

"Juliet Niner Zero, regroup and continue the advance," Bull ordered, realizing that time had taken on an even greater importance.

"What about the wounded?" Smyth retorted rebelliously.

Bull started to tell him to give the wounded to the sergeant major, but couldn't remember the sergeant major's callsign.

"This is Bravo Two Victor Niner Zero. We'll take the wounded," a voice said.

If you believe that this is Sergeant Major Ogren, turn to section 135.

If you don't believe that this is the sergeant major, turn to section 136.

— 119 —

The rest of the trip to phaseline Amber was long but uneventful. Bull's panzers sniffed out the terrain just ahead of the skimmers, which were constantly nudged by the fast softskinned vehicles. To their right they passed endless fields, some being harvested by worried farmers, others empty and untouched since the last battle of the war against the Crageens and Jebbitt's Raiders.

Bull grunted to himself, thinking that they still were fighting the last battle with Jebbitt's Raiders. This battle was for keeps, with the lives of the Raiders balanced against the survival of Hammer's regiment. Bull had no illusions about that. Enough of the Slammers' tanks and skimmers had gone down in the transport *Vindictive* that Colonel Hammer might not be able to fulfill his next contract. If the Raiders defeated Bull, Jebbitt would come for Hammer's head and massacre the few Slammers remaining on Maffren. Equipped with Slammer tanks and skimmers, the Raiders would easily crush the remaining forces Colonel Hammer could field.

"They mean to finish us," Sergeant Major Ogren said suddenly, reflecting Bromley's thoughts. No one replied.

Just before Bull's tank entered the town of Tooey, two buzzbombs roared out at him. Timmons jerked the controls and forced the huge blower to the right.

"Return fire," Bull ordered. He had no need; the tanks on either side of him had already opened up.

The enemy has two infantry squads in the town. Each squad has an Ordnance value of 2. They are well set up and attack using Chart C.

The Slammers also attack using Chart C.

If the Slammers are destroyed, turn to section 29.

If the enemy withdraws or is destroyed, turn to section 121.

— 120 —

The long trek to the next phaseline disturbed Lieutenant Bromley. He hated the need to be in the rear; he had always believed in leading from the front. But the open plains were best scouted by skimmers. The support of two tanks to each skimmer platoon was the best guarantee Bull could provide that any enemy assault on the lightly armored skimmers would be, at the very least, ill-advised, if not plain fatal.

As it was, Bull's decision proved wise. Pete Smyth suggested and Bull ordered the two flanking platoons to pincer the phaseline. It worked well. On the phaseline were two infantry squads, dug in and ready to fight. Bull's tanks roared first.

The enemy has two infantry squads in the town. Each squad has an Ordnance value of 2. They fight using Chart D.

The Slammers fight using Chart B.

If the enemy destroys the Slammers, turn to section 29.

If the enemy is destroyed or withdraws, turn to section 122.

— 121 —

The roar of buzzbombs startled Bull into the realization that he had no artillery to call on. He couldn't expect the buzzbombs to be neutralized by Central's all-seeing computers. He was on his own.

Timmons jerked the tank to the left and then to the right, deftly dodging two buzzbombs. A sudden unplanned jerk, a loud explosion and accompanying brilliance told Bull that Timmons hadn't dodged all the buzzbombs. For a moment he thought they were done for, then the great tank shook itself and eased forward, a vicious, glowing scar along its flank displaying where the enemy had almost been lucky enough. The powergun flashed out and licked the town. Beside him, other tanks blasted the town. To his rear and rapidly fanning out, smaller arms fire from the infantry platoons deftly dealt with the enemy.

Timmons dodged one more buzzbomb and then it was over. The enemy had either retreated or been obliterated.

"Get your wounded to Victor Niner Zero," Bull called to his command, warning the sergeant major to be ready to accept more Slammer wounded.

"Phaseline Amber secured," Lieutenant Dyer said, reporting the obvious.

Amber. Next to Gold and finally Iridium. They were still far but maybe not too late. He had to reform the order of march for the last leg of their mission.

If Combat Group Foxtrot should position the skimmer platoons just in front of the tanks, turn to section 51.

If the combat group should send the tanks forward to recon, turn to section 54.

— 122 —

The enemy's response was good enough for his strength but not good enough for Hammer's Slammers. Red tongues of energy licked the town and tore through the enemy's positions. A few of the enemy replied and had some effect on the Slammers, but Bull's panzers spoke with authority. Bull's infantry secured the smoldering ruins of phaseline Amber, the town of Tooey.

While the skimmers searched through the town for any signs of further resistance, Lieutenant Bromley grappled with the problem of the next movement. Over thirty kays lay between Tooey and phaseline Gold. Not more than seven kays lay between Gold and Iridium, the beleaguered Slammers at the wreck. But those thirty kays worried Bull.

If Bull chooses to continue moving in the same formation, turn to section 51.

If Bull chooses to move with his tank platoons in far recon, turn to section 54.

— 123 —

"Foxtrot, execute Bluejay Five," Bull ordered, tapping Sara on her helmet. His fourth display flickered and switched to reveal the CEOI callsigns. As leader of Combat Group One his personal callsign was N4M20.

"November Four Mike, this is Mike Two Zero," Bull called.

"Alpha Six Juliet Niner Zero," Lieutenant Smyth replied.

"We're charging through you; fade back," Bull informed him, then called to Dyer, "November Niner Zero, attack through Foxtrot."

"Roger," came the reply.

Together, the two tank platoons forged through the skimmers. The enemy fire grew more frantic but less effective.

The enemy has four tanks in the woods, each with an Ordnance value of 2. They attack using Chart D. The enemy withdraws after three rounds of combat.

The Slammers attack using Chart B.

If the enemy destroys the Slammers, turn to section 29.

If the enemy is defeated or withdraws, turn to section 125.

— 124 —

"We're compromised!" Ennis groaned. "They've got our frequency; they know our battle plan!"

"This is Foxtrot, execute emergency CEOI. Foxtrot out," Engles said over the radio calmly. To Lieutenant Bromley she said, "The display for the CEOI is on screen four, sir."

"Roger," Bull replied, but he had no time to look at it. "Get me Smyth."

"Alpha Six Juliet Niner Zero, this is November Fower Mike Two Zero Alpha, over," Sara radioed. Bull found time to marvel at Engles's ability to memorize the various callsigns of the emergency CEOIs while he glanced over at the display.

"This is Alpha Six Juliet Niner Zero," Smyth replied.

"Have you got everyone?" Bull asked immediately.

"Negative. We don't have Kilo Fower Charlie," Smyth replied.

"Forget him. Just change the plan; they're wise to us," Bull snapped. Ennis lobbed another shot at the forest.

The enemy has four tanks in the forest. Each tank has an Ordnance value of 2. They have surprised the Slammers and forced them to switch their tactics. The enemy attacks using Chart B. They withdraw after three rounds of combat.

The Slammers attack using Chart D.

If the Slammers are destroyed, turn to section 29.

If the enemy withdraws or is destroyed, turn to section 125.

— 125 —

The enemy was outgunned, outclassed, and shortly, they were dead. Dust, dirt, and debris rose over mounds of twisted metal and torn flesh. It had been hot work, and Bull had to wipe his face with his kerchief to keep his binoculars from slipping. He swore at the sight of shattered skimmers while Timmons swapped insults with Gleeson's driver concerning the way she managed to get two new scars on her tank.

"You'd better get a bandage for that wound!" Timmons jeered.

"Nothing a case of beer won't cure," she returned.

"Enough," Bull said over the intercom to Timmons. He knew that his driver had a thing going with Gleeson's, but he needed his platoon to hear him, not two love birds.

"November Fower Mike, Mike Two Zero," Bull called on the regiment's frequency. "Advance to phaseline Amber."

"Roger," Lieutenant Smyth replied. "Leaving the wounded for—" He stopped, realizing that he didn't know what to call the softskinned section.

If you think that the callsign for Sergeant Major Ogren and the softskinned vehicles is W3Y90A, turn to section 66.

If you think it's something else, turn to section 65.

— 126 —

"Roger," Engles replied. "Foxtrot switching . . . *now*!" All the while, Bull trained his weapon on the oncoming missile. Careful! Careful! he said to himself, steady—now! With a short burst Lieutenant Bromley's turret gun flamed blue-green onto the head of the oncoming missile. Flame and a sudden, loud explosion told him he'd hit.

"I don't believe it!" Ennis exclaimed, but Bull wasn't listening. "Dodge the other one!" he roared at Timmons.

"Righto!" Timmons replied gamely, slithering the huge tank in a stomach-wrenching maneuver.

"Mike Two Zero this is Juliet Niner Zero," the voice of Smyth demanded.

"She's yours if this gets me!" Bull replied quickly. The missile sped closer, and suddenly a dull roar and a brilliant flare told Bull—

—that he was still alive. Along the length of the tank glowed a huge score mark, all that remained of the fury of a warhead that had hit just off its aim. They were alive.

"Continue toward the phaseline," Bull told Timmons.

Now he had a chance to look around. The two infantry platoons were moving against light fire and would soon reach the edge of the village.

The enemy has two squads of infantry in the village with an Ordnance value of 2 each. They attack using Chart D.

The Slammers attack using Chart B.

If the enemy destroys the Slammers, turn to section 29.

If the enemy is destroyed or retreats, turn to section 128.

— 127 —

"We're compromised!" Engles barked. "The enemy's on our frequency."

With the enemy on Group Foxtrot's frequency, everything Bull said and was said to him would instantly be overheard. The effects would be devastating. Normally such things would never happen—the Slammers had laserlink communications that could not be intercepted unless the enemy captured a Slammer radio. Colonel Hammer thought about such things and ensured that each unit had emergency CEOIs. Unfortunately, the enemy had them, too. Bull's only hope was that the enemy didn't know about their emergency CEOIs and the emergency frequencies they detailed.

"Turn to the emergency frequency." Bull never remembered saying it, so intently was he concentrating on the oncoming missiles. A freak hit from Ennis got the farther one, and Timmons made a frantic effort to turn the tank out of the path of the other missile.

A screech and a roar. The whole world lit up and then went black.

When Bull's eyes readjusted, he discovered he was still alive. A brilliant white line running the length of the tank told him that Timmons had turned just enough to deflect the missile. The score mark was deep enough to tell Bull that Timmons's turn had been barely enough.

"Good work, Greg!" Bull yelled. "You get a case for that one!"

"It was coming right at me!" Timmons grumbled. "What'd you expect me to do?"

Around them the battle raged on. Bull's tank was much closer now, following the age-old tradition of moving toward an ambush. The two flanking infantry platoons had grounded and were heading toward the village on foot, encountering what Bull thought to be a surprisingly small amount of fire.

The enemy has two infantry squads in the city with an Ordnance value of 1 each. They attack using Chart C.

The Slammers also attack using Chart C.

If Group Foxtrot is destroyed, turn to section 29.

If the enemy is destroyed or retreats, turn to section 128.

— 128 —

The two squads of enemy infantry were no match for Bull's skimmer-mounted professionals. They fought hard for a short time, then broke and scattered before the onslaught. Smyth's platoon secured the phaseline and cared for its wounded. Peyton's platoon pressed on a bit, sending back its wounded, as did Bravo India.

"We move in two mikes," Bull told his command, meaning that they would move in two minutes. That gave him a very short one hundred twenty seconds in which to decide what formation to use for their last major movement before they reached the wreck. The road ahead stretched thirty kilometers to phaseline Gold. Then it was a scant six kilometers more to the wreck itself. The terrain nagged at him. He had to decide which formation to use, and he had to decide now.

If Lieutenant Bromley decides to send his infantry ahead of his tanks, turn to section 51.

If Lieutenant Bromley decides to send his tanks ahead in a forward recon, turn to section 54.

— 129 —

"Switch to emergency CEOI," Bull decided. Engles glanced at him sharply. "Yes, I know the enemy has them as well, but they have to think of it first, and they don't know our strength." I hope, Bull added to himself.

"Foxtrot, Bluejay Five!" Engles said over the radio. "The bird has squawked. Out." To the lieutenant she added, "Switching frequencies. The callsigns are on your fourth display."

Bull grunted thanks and peered at the new and unfamiliar callsigns. The Slammers rarely used the CEOIs; they existed only for emergencies like this one. His callsign as group commander was—

If you think that Lieutenant Bromley's callsign as combat group commander is November Fower Mike Two Zero, turn to section 131.

If you think that November Fower Mike Two Zero is not Lieutenant Bromley's combat group commander callsign, turn to section 132.

— 130 —

"Bluejay Five. The bird has squawked," Bull agreed. He nodded to Sara, who switched to the code frequencies they had passed out earlier. Bull punched up the new callsigns on his fourth display.

"November Four Mike, this is Mike Two Zero," he called to his command. To his platoon he said, "Zulu Ate Golf, this is Golf Niner Zero."

As Sara fielded the replies from Bull's platoon, Bull switched back to the combat group frequency.

"This is Alpha Six Juliet Niner Zero," Smyth replied.

"Roger. How many of those buzzbombs did your guys capture?" Bull asked hurriedly.

"Enough," Smyth replied. "I reckon they're in the woods."

"Me, too. Are your men up to it?" Bull asked.

"Give the word."

"We'll be right behind you," Bull replied. "Go to it."

"Alpha Six Juliet, this is Juliet Niner Zero. Big Daddy has said that we can play with the meanies," Smyth told the rest of the infantry.

"Wow!" "Whoopee!" "Hubba, hubba!" the others cheered.

"Now, did you all get those toys from the other boys?" Smyth continued in the same vein. "Be prepared to use them." Then he got serious. "Juliet, advance."

Ahead of him Bull could see groups of skimmers flit around the fork in the road and head carefully for the forest ahead. He knew that the noise of his tank's blower might give the attack away, so he waited impatiently.

The first roar of a buzzbomb was all he needed. "Attack!"

The enemy has four hovertanks, each of Ordnance value 2. They attack using Chart D and withdraw after three rounds of combat.

The Slammers attack using Chart B.

If the enemy destroys the Slammers, turn to section 29.

If the enemy withdraws or is destroyed, turn to section 133.

— 131 —

"November Fower Mike, this is November Fower Mike Two Zero," Bull called to his units.

"This is Alpha Six Juliet Niner Zero," Pete Smyth replied. "Suggestions?"

"They look like the sort of thing you'd better deal with," Lieutenant Peyton replied.

"Roger," Bull agreed. "Kilo Six November Niner Zero, this is Mike Two Zero."

"This is November Niner Zero," Dyer replied.

"Engage the enemy by platoon bounds," Bull ordered. Platoon bounds meant that one platoon would advance while the other fired, then they would change off as the moving platoon got into a closer position to the enemy.

"Request permission to open fire," Dyer replied, wisely realizing that Bull would decide to move first.

"On my mark." To his own platoon Bull said, "Zulu Ate Golf this is Golf Niner Zero. Prepare to maneuver by bounds. On the mark—*mark*!" Bull toggled his radio to transmit to both his platoon and Dyer.

Immediately, Dyer's platoon opened fire on the enemy position while Bull's platoon roared toward the enemy, guns silent.

The enemy has four hovertanks, each of Ordnance value 4. The enemy attacks using Chart D and withdraws after three rounds of combat.

The Slammers attack using Chart B.

If the enemy destroys the Slammers, turn to section 29.

If the Slammers destroy or drive off the enemy, turn to section 133.

— 132 —

You're wrong. Only static answers. Turn to section 131 and take time to examine the Communications Equipment Operating Instructions in the appendix of this novel before you get more Slammers killed!

— 133 —

The enemy didn't have a chance. Bull's Slammers were tired and bloodied, but they wanted revenge for the dead they'd left behind, and they got it. In short order the enemy was either dead or fled. Bull couldn't tell which because there was nothing left of the forest. Infantry and tankers argued momentarily about who had destroyed what, and Bull let them. He had to think.

They had secured phaseline White. The next phaseline was Gold, then Iridium. But the road to Gold went through a wide-open stretch that had cover for the enemy six and seven kilometers from the road—within easy range of guns but well hidden from binoculars. Bull's decision had to be the right one or there would be no more Slammers.

If Lieutenant Bromley decides to keep his group together, with the hovertanks as a shield and the infantry in front of the softskinneds, turn to section 68.

If Lieutenant Bromley chooses to continue sending his infantry in far recon in front of his panzers and the softskinneds, turn to section 69.

— 134 —

"Negative," Bull replied. "We'll do it together." He turned to glance back at the rest of his command. "November Fower Mike, secure phaseline Iridium." Cheers and catcalls filled the airwaves as Combat Group Foxtrot moved forward.

Ahead of them the wreck spread out, fallen mainly to the right. Bull suspected that the blast had been on its left side. "Steer right," Bull ordered. Moving in unison, skimmers and tanks together, the battle-tried command moved toward the fighting.

"I have a tank engaging the wreck," Smyth called.

"Wait," Bull replied, scanning the same scene. "Ennis, put a round just in front of him. Then burn him if he doesn't do a jackrabbit."

The first shot landed in front of the moving hovertank and brought it up sharp as its commander searched the terrain for his assailant. Bull could see the commander jump as he spotted Foxtrot and gesticulate wildly. It must have been too much for one of the pongoes; a well-aimed shot took the commander's head off his shoulders. After that it was over.

Bull's command met up with the fighting survivors in short order and proceeded to secure the area around the loading bay where the hovertanks had been stowed. In five minutes they had ten tanks righted and crewed, charging out after an enemy that was rapidly running out of ammunition and options. Behind Bull's impromptu tank company was another company of skimmers, led by Smyth, which skittered behind the tanks clearing up pockets of enemy infantry. Farther behind, Sergeant Major Ogren began the weary, sad task of getting the medical supplies to the wounded.

Two hours later there was no enemy. A final push had caught Colonel Gesparde Jebbitt and the remnants of his command staff in a stolen combat car fleeing from the desperate battle. Bull thought to himself that all he ever got to fight were big battles against a desperate Jebbitt.

"I demand to be treated in accordance with the rules of war," Jebbitt proclaimed in a surly voice.

"Sure, just like the plains of Tegara," Smyth retorted.

"Steady," Bull said calmingly. To Jebbitt he said, "The authorities of Maffren will be more than glad to deal with your pleas." The little colonel paled and wilted.

Turn to section 137.

— 135 —

"Roger," Smyth acknowledged. "We'll be ready to move out shortly."

Bull glanced over the torn terrain, eyes passing over the lifeless eyes of men who had moments before been very much alive. Overhead, the sun beat down. Bull thought that he could see birds approaching in the far distance. Maybe they weren't buzzards or even true birds, but they served the same purpose on this world—to scavenge the dead. With a dull ache, Bull realized that he had a choice: preserve the sanctity of the dead or ensure the survival of the living.

"November Fower Mike, this is Mike Two Zero," Bull said, deciding on his action. "This new information about our enemy means that he had some hand in bringing down the transport. He knew where it was going to fall and when. He must be there now, trying to get more of our equipment. But he has to kill Slammers to do it, and he must be finding that awfully hard. We press on immediately. Two Zero out."

It wasn't Bull's best speech, but he never was really good at them. He frowned and worried that the men under him might damn him for being heartless, leaving the dead to be ravaged by more than energy bolts.

Smyth's voice broke Bull's thoughts. "Mike Two Zero, Juliet Niner Zero. Moving at this time."

"November Niner Zero, ready to move," Dyer said, adding "champing at the bit."

"Alpha Niner Zero moving!"

"Charlie Niner Zero on the way!"

"Victor Niner Zero, on your tail, Mike," the Sergeant Major roared. Bull swiveled around and saw that Ogren had detached a small group to look after the wounded. They would catch up well before the rest of the softskinneds moved out.

With a rush of feeling, Bull realized that his men understood his reasoning. There were Slammers out there fighting for their life; the dead had no such worries.

The forward platoon edged past the forest on their left, moving to the edge of the lake on the right. Here the woods ended and a wide plain opened up. Their road turned to the right into a gentle curve that entered the next town.

Peyton's platoon fanned to the left to brush against the wide hill north of the forest, while Bravo India swept over the lake and to the far side. Smyth's platoon was in the lead.

If you have written ''Smyth'' on your notepaper, turn to section 22.

If you did not write ''Smyth,'' turn to section 138.

— 136 —

''Who is that?'' Bull called imperiously.
''The sergeant major,'' Sara Engles replied calmly.
Bull blushed and shut up.

Turn to section 135.

— 137 —

''At ease, dammit!'' Colonel Alois Hammer snapped. ''You two look like peacocks on parade.'' His eyes impaled Bromley. ''You think you did very well, don't you?'' Hammer slapped his desk with a folder. ''These are the dead.'' With another folder: ''These are the lost skimmers.'' Another folder: ''The lost tanks.''

Under the withering attack, Pete Smyth broke his stance had started to speak. ''Be quiet!'' Hammer snapped. Smyth's jaw snapped shut. Then something in Hammer's manner changed. "Why'd you two fight, anyway?"

Bull's stomach turned over. He didn't say anything. "Well?" Hammer's word turned like a dagger in the air. Bull pursed his lips, forcing them to stay closed. Smyth was looking at a point in the air just above Hammer's right shoulder.

"Via, I know it was over a girl!" Hammer barked. "So speak!" A ruckus outside disturbed him. He could hear loud voices, and then the door opened—when Colonel Hammer hadn't ordered it. Smyth and Bromley rotated to glance at the open door in time to see a woman hit a man where he can never defend himself and burst through the door. It was Donna Mills.

"And just what do you think you're doing?" Hammer asked pleasantly, but with dark overtones.

"I was about to ask you the same," Donna snapped back. "Just what is going on here?"

Hammer sighed. "I was trying to find out what these two 'officers' "—and he stressed the word to imply that this was a conditional rank—"were doing brawling over a woman." With an appraising glance that almost made Donna blush, Hammer added, "I see now that they both have good taste."

"Enough!" Bull barked. There were some things he wouldn't take from any officer.

Hammer glanced up at him coldly. "You were saying?" Hammer prodded.

Bull glanced at Smyth. With a shrug he said, "I had been trying to tell Lieutenant Smyth that he should quit the Slammers"—Smyth gave him a startled glance—"and marry this lady, but I had to tell her first."

"Quit the Slammers?" Donna's tone was puzzled and incredulous.

"Indeed." Hammer agreed. "That is quite something to say to another officer."

Bull shrugged. "He's learned enough, but his heart's not in it. One day he'd be thinking too much or too little, and that'd be the end of him." Defensively he added, "He's a fine officer and a good soldier, but he shouldn't stay with the Slammers, he should stay here. With Donna."

Smyth was agitated now. Hammer's expression was indecipherable, while Donna Mills bore the expression of one who had been both betrayed and saved at the same time.

"I am surprised to hear you say that," Alois Hammer began dangerously, "but I agree with you." He turned to Smyth. "You are under no obligation, and could rejoin at any time, but as Lieutenant Bromley has so poorly put it, you don't need to be in this job."

Smyth was taken aback. "But sir, I've no qualifications for other work, no job, no—"

"You're a Slammer," Hammer replied firmly. "The Maffrens will take you with a bump or two in rank. A captain leaving the Slammers would be a colonel in the Maffren forces. Of course, I could give you a commission as an agent as well." Hammer glanced at one of the folders he had previously slammed onto the table. Caught out, he grinned and explained, "Your personnel folder. You're qualified in at least three professions, but if I were to guess, I'd say you'll be a politician in no time."

Smyth looked inquiringly at Bull, who grunted and said, "Do I have to hit you again?" Donna grabbed Smyth's hand.

"Get out of here!" Hammer roared at the confused lieutenant. "Get out and draw your pay." In a softer tone he added, "If it doesn't work out, you can come back—Captain!"

A dazed Peter Smyth allowed himself to be pulled out of the room by a determined Donna Mills.

"Now," Hammer continued, "I believe there is still a charge of assaulting a fellow officer against you." Bull turned back sharply and came to attention. "You have that on your record, and I won't erase it. But you're a fighter, Bromley. You'll stay in and prove to me that you hit that man for a good reason. Won't you?"

Bull thought. He'd seen enough fighting, blood, and spilled guts. He didn't need it anymore. But something . . . something always nagged at him. Yeah, he'd stay.

"Why?" Hammer snarled, seeing Bull's reaction.

Bull looked up right into Hammer's eyes. He looked through them and tried to pierce into the mind behind. Failing that, he told the truth.

"We've been lucky," Bull said. "I think that one day we're going to meet some other intelligence bigger, faster, stronger, and meaner than ours." He paused. "Mother Nature's never played favorites. Not on Earth, not in the stars." He looked for a reaction from Hammer but didn't get it. "There's going to be something out there one day that'll fight and fight and won't give quarter until we show it that we can either lick it or we're beaten by it." He spread his hands. "This—this is just keeping in practice."

"You *kill* for practice?" Hammer asked.

"Don't you?"

THE END

— 138 —

Ahead, Pete Smyth kept a vigilant watch for any signs of the enemy. There were two towns close together on the road, separated by a bit of forest. Beyond that the road looped west around a mountain and due north into another small woods. Towns, woods, mountain, woods, hill to the west—they were all ideal spots for potential ambushes.

The second town worried Pete Smyth the most. That and maybe the woods due north. They were a great place to cover several approaches to the wreck. His stomach churning with worry, Smyth grounded his skimmer and scanned the horizon with his binoculars.

Look at the picture on the next page.

If you think that the terrain is clear, turn to section 110.

If you think that the terrain should be investigated, turn to section 111.

APPENDIX A

FOR YOUR EYES ONLY

The following is the organization of the 1st combat Group organized as the combat element for the relief convoy dispatched to the wreck of the special transport *Vindictive*.

Place a pencil check in the box for each unit if it is destroyed.

COMBAT GROUP FOXTROT
Commander: 1LT Braddington Bromley
2nd in Command: 2LT Peter Smyth
Senior NCO: CSM Ogren

Foxtrot Alpha Tango
2nd Platoon, 1st Tank Co.
Training Unit
2LT (prov) Martin Dyer
4 hovertanks

☐	☐	☐	☐
FAT16	FAT18	FAT24	FAT20
2LT	Sgt.	Sgt.	SFC
Dyer	Hopkins	Roberts	Biddle

Ordnance: 4
Stealth: 4

Foxtrot India
1st Platoon, 1st Infantry Co.
Combat-Experienced Unit
2LT Peter Smyth
4 squads of 10 skimmers
jeep and mortar elements detached

☐	☐	☐	☐
R16	R18	R24	R20
2LT	Sgt.	Sgt.	SFC
Smyth	Redpath	White	Beirne

Ordnance: 2
Stealth: 8

Foxtrot Tango
1st Platoon, 1st Tank Co.
Combat-Experienced Unit
1LT Braddington Bromley
4 hovertanks

☐	☐	☐	☐
L26	L28	L24	L20
1LT	Sgt.	Sgt.	SFC
Bromley	Gleeson	Healey	Lewis

Ordnance: 4
Stealth: 4

Foxtrot Alpha India
2nd Platoon, 1st Infantry Co.
Training Unit
2LT (prov) Morris Peyton
4 squads of 10 skimmers
(jeep and mortar elements detached)

FATI16	FAI18	FAI14	FAI10
2LT	Sgt.		SFC
Peyton	Hill	Freeman	Stodnick

Ordnance: 2
Stealth: 8

Foxtrot Bravo India
3rd Platoon, 1st Infantry Co.
Training Unit
2LT (prov) Jeric Johnson
4 squads of 10 skimmers
(jeep and mortar elements detached)

FAB16	FAB28	FAB24	FAB20
2LT	Sgt.	Sgt.	SFC
Johnson	Madrigal	Greer	Santy

Ordnance: 2
Stealth: 8

Sierra Major
Wheeled Relief Column
Ad Hoc Unit
CSM Ogren
70 wheeled vehicles of various types, many acquired from the general populace. Vehicles are loaded with medical supplies, equipment, and personnel. Standard Hammer's Regiment side arms for all field medical personnel. Vehicles driven by Replacement Section personnel equipped with standard-issue weapons.

Combat value: negligible
Stealth: 4

APPENDIX B

HAMMER'S REGIMENT

COMMUNICATIONS EQUIPMENT OPERATING INSTRUCTIONS

The callsign of a unit is determined by examining its position within the tables listed below. The third tank of the first platoon of the first company tank battalion would have callsign: Z8G12. The commander of the vehicle would identify himself as: Z8G12Y while the radio operator would be Z8G12A. Other personnel in the vehicle would use the vehicle's callsign. The same procedure is followed for infantry and combat cars.

Units detached to form a combat group platoon squad use the same callsigns as the sub unit designators for their respective branch. The 2nd Tank Company of a combat group would identify itself as U2X. An entire unit is referred to by its callsign, a sub-element is referred to by that callsign with the appropriate suffix added. Thus, the commander of the 2nd Tank Company would be U2X90 while his radio operator would be U2X90A.

For pronunciation, see the section *The Phonetic Alphabet*.

COMMUNICATIONS PROCEDURES

The commanding unit initiates the network. Thus, the commander (or his radio operator) of the 1st Platoon, 2nd Infantry Company initiates contact with the rest of his unit. When communicating with the company commander or other elements, the platoon leader uses his full callsign for initial contact but may then revert to an abbreviated callsign.

Example of joining 2nd Infantry Company's net:

Company Commander: "Juliet One Foxtrot, this is Juliet One Foxtrot Niner Zero. Over."

(First Platoon leader replies.)

Second Platoon leader replies: "Juliet One Foxtrot, this is Alpha Two Alpha Niner Zero. Request to join the net."

Company Commander: "Alpha Niner Zero, this is Foxtrot Niner Zero. Time is Zero One Two Twenty Golf Mike Tango."

(Third Platoon leader replies.)

(Fourth Platoon leader replies.)

CONFIDENTIAL   CONFIDENTIAL
               HAMMER'S REGIMENT

UNIT CALLSIGNS

B4I	Regiment
C9Q	Headquarters Battalion
D2N	Combat Cars Battalion
E3L	Tank Battalion
F5H	Infantry Battalion
G8P	Regimental Artillery
Z1O	Regimental Replacement Battalion
N4M	1st Combat Group/Platoon/Squad
W9B	2nd Combat Group/Platoon/Squad
O6C	3rd Combat Group/Platoon/Squad
T2K	Tactical Operations Center (TOC)
20	Commander of Regiment/Battalion/Group/TOC

SUB-UNIT CALLSIGNS

W3Y		1st Company, Tank Battalion
	Z8G	1st Platoon
	K6N	2nd Platoon
	B2V	3rd Platoon
	Z3K	4th Platoon
U2X		2nd Company, Tank Battalion
N2Z		3rd Company, Tank Battalion
O2E		4th Company, Tank Battalion
A6J		1st Company, Infantry Battalion
	G1B	1st Platoon
	A2A	2nd Platoon
	K4C	3rd Platoon
	L6D	4th Platoon
J1F		2nd Company, Infantry Battalion
V7R		3rd Company, Infantry Battalion
H3T		4th Company, Infantry Battalion
90		Platoon Leader
24		1st Squad/Tank
36		2nd Squad/Tank
12		3rd Squad/Tank
14		4th Squad /Tank
A		Radio Operator
Y		Commander of Squad/Tank

CONFIDENTIAL   CONFIDENTIAL
HAMMER'S REGIMENT

UNIT CALLSIGNS

B4I Regiment/C9Q Headquarters Battalion/D2N Combat Cars Battalion/E3L Tank Battalion/F5H Infantry Battalion/ G8P Regimental Artillery/Z10 Regimental Replacement Battalion/N4M 1st Combat Group/Platoon/Squad/W9B 2nd Combat Group/Platoon/Squad/O6C 3rd Combat Group/Platoon/Squad/ T2K Tactical Operations Center (TOC)/20 Regiment/Battalion/ Group/TOC Commander

SUB-UNIT CALLSIGNS

1st Tank Company W3Y:
W3Y 1st Company, Tank Battalion/U2X 2nd Company, Tank Battalion/N2Z 3rd Company, Tank Battalion/O2E 4th Company, Tank Battalion
1st Infantry Company A6F
A6J 1st Company, Infantry Battalion/J1F 2nd Company, Infantry Battalion/V7R 3rd Company, Infantry Battalion/H3T 4th Company, Infantry Battalion
1st Platoon Z8G/2nd Platoon K6N/3rd Platoon B2V/4th Platoon Z3K
1st Platoon G1B/2nd Platoon A2A/3rd Platoon K4C/4th Platoon L6D
Platoon Leader 90/1st Squad/Tank 24/2nd Squad/Tank 36/3rd Squad/Tank 12/4th Squad/Tank 14
Radio Operator A/Squad/Tank Commander Y

THE PHONETIC ALPHABET

A	Alpha	N	November
B	Bravo	O	Oscar
C	Charlie	P	Papa
D	Delta	Q	Quebec
E	Echo	R	Romeo
F	Foxtrot	S	Sierra
G	Golf	T	Tango
H	Hotel	U	Uniform
I	India	V	Victor
J	Juliet	W	Whiskey
K	Kilo	X	X-ray
L	Lariat	Y	Yankee
M	Mike	Z	Zulu

1	One	6	Six
2	Two	7	Seven
3	Tree	8	Ate
4	Fower	9	Niner
5	Fife	0	Zero

Note: Numbers are pronounced as written. This enables clear communication over excessive static or jamming.

APPENDIX C

WAR PLANS

PHASELINES FOR OPERATION RUNNING DOG

NOTE: Phaselines are an emergency exigency used only when satellite communications and control have been removed for unforeseen circumstances. Phaselines are used to ensure that all elements of a command are in the same general position or that the terrain up to and including a phaseline has been secured.

Central Route (Northwest):

Yellow	– 1st Tee Junction
Aqua	– the town of Plains
Green	– the city of Heatherlake
Amber	– the town of Tooey
Gold	– the town of Regarra
Iridium	– the survivors of the wreck

Lower Route (West North):

Orange	– 1st Tee Junction
Aqua	– the town of Plains
Red	– the town of Smithtown
Amber	– the town of Tooey
Gold	– the town of Regarra
Iridium	– the survivors of the wreck

Upper Route (North West):

Indigo	– the town of Lakeside
Fawn	– the town of Glendale
Lavender	– the village of Cullea
Rust	– the village of Nickel Run
Blue	– the 2nd fork junction after Nickel Run
Brown	– the 1st tee junction after Nickel Run
White	– the 2nd tee junction after Nickel Run
Gold	– the town of Regarra
Iridium	– the survivors of the wreck

Additional phaselines:

Copper	– the town of Gold City
Pink	– the village of Hillstart

CONFIDENTIAL 1 CONFIDENTIAL

APPENDIX D

GLOSSARY OF COMMON MILITARY TERMS AND SLANG

Several abbreviations have been adopted into use in the military over the millennia, and several non-standard words have crept into the vocabulary of the mercenaries. Here is a brief list with meanings:

APC: Armored Personnel Carrier

airwaves: an old reference to the days of radio communication. Nowadays, communication is by direct laserlink

azimuth: a degree measurement, with North normally taken as zero degrees

blitz: shortening of blitzkrieg

blitzkrieg: German—literally "lightning war"

buzzards: slang term for buzzbomb-equipped infantry

buzzbomb: name given to an anti-tank missile. Buzzbombs are usually limited to very short ranges because satellite surveillance can detect their launch and destroy them before they reach their targets. From exceedingly close range, however, not even a computer can react quickly enough to save a tank.

bomb report: report submitted upon detecting a bombing by the enemy. Normally not necessary, owing to satellite surveillance.

callsign: letters and numbers used to designate a unit, particularly in the late twentieth century, when only unsecure radio communication was available

CEOI: Communications Equipment Operating Instruction. CEOIs are books containing general radio/laser usage information as well as several coding guides and the callsigns for various units of a command. In the late twentieth century callsigns were assigned in such a manner that the enemy would not be able to determine the composition of the unit, and the callsigns were changed frequently (sometimes more often than every twenty-four hours) to deny the enemy the chance to gather intelligence. Nowadays, CEOI callsigns are rarely used except in extraordinary circumstances.

comm.: short for communications

commo: normally used to apply to communications gear

comlink: communications link

Crageen: inhabitant of the Crag mountains or their immediate vicinity. Also used to describe any offspring of an inhabitant of the Crag mountains.

dat: Dumb-assed Tanker. Used by suicidal pongoes.

dats: plural of DAT

footslogger: see *Pongo*

freq: short for frequency. Different frequencies are used by sub-elements of each command. A platoon has a different frequency than a company, and a company's frequency differs from the battalion's.

groundcar: four-wheeled vehicle that moves by direct contact with the ground

groundtank: tracked tank that moves by direct contact with the ground

grunt: slang name for an infantryman. See *pongo*.

Guderian: General Heinz Guderian, famed as the originator of modern combined arms tactics. His Panzer Corps broke through the French at Sedan in the Second World War, thereby revolutionizing the art of war.

hovertank: a tank that rides on a cushion of air

infrared: use of the infrared wavelengths to detect the heat given off by objects, particularly tanks

IR: commonly used abbreviation for infrared

iridium: very strong metal used for armoring combat vehicles.

jink: term used to describe the dodging maneuvers of tanks under fire. First used by Guderian to describe the actions of German tanks dodging Russian tanks.

kay: kilometer

laserlink: laser communications link. A tight-focused laser beam which cannot be intercepted by any enemy. However, anyone equipped with reception gear on the proper frequency can receive the communications. Thus it is important not to lose functioning receivers to the enemy.

Lt.: common abbreviation for Lieutenant

NCO: Non-Commissioned Officer

net: slang for network. A combat element communicates in a communications network. Management of this network is vital in war for fast, efficient communication.

panzer: German word for tank

phaseline: line drawn on a map used as a reference line for the positioning of troops. With satellite surveillance and on-board computers, phaselines are usually unnecessary.

pongo (plural: pongoes): slang term for an infantryman

powerpack: engine and transmission unit of a vehicle

powerbolt: energy bolt shot by a powergun

powergun: gun that utilizes a special property of metal powders in magnetic fields to produce a bolt of uni-directional pure energy

push: slang for frequency

roger: Used in communications to say: "I heard your last message and understand it."

sar'major: common mispronunciation of the rank sergeant major, the highest non-commissioned officer rank

sitrep: situation report, a report that includes status of men, equipment, ammunition, supplies, and enemy position

softskinned: something without armor, normally referring to a groundtruck or groundcar

spot report: report submitted upon detecting an enemy or an unusual (possibly enemy-inspired) event

tribarrel: Powerguns generate intense fringe heat, and so barrels could not be used for extended periods of time. One method of maintaining a high rate of fire is to employ three barrels centered on a common axis, rotating each barrel for cooling after firing through it.

wilco: Used in communications to say "will comply." Wilco also implies that a person has heard and understood the command with which he/she is complying, thus wilco also means "roger, will comply."

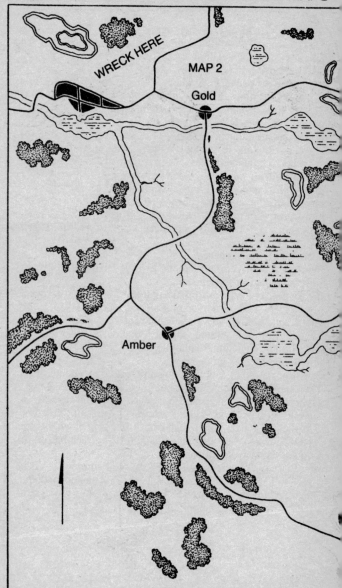

COLOR CODES (CEOI'S)

Yellow

Blue

MAP 6

Copper

Rust

MAP 3

MAP 4

Lavender

P.

Green

Fawn

MAP 5

Aqua

Yellow Orange

MAP 1

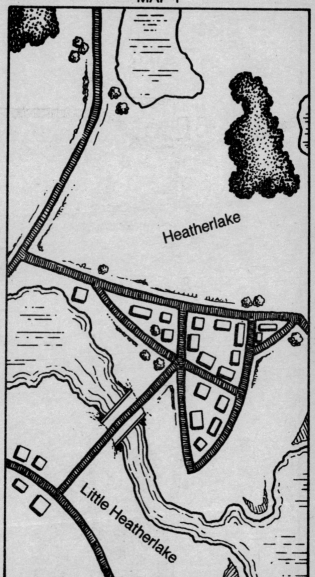

Heatherlake

Little Heatherlake

MAP 2

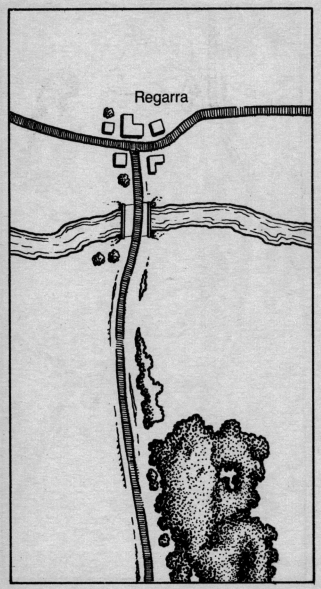

Regarra

MAP 3

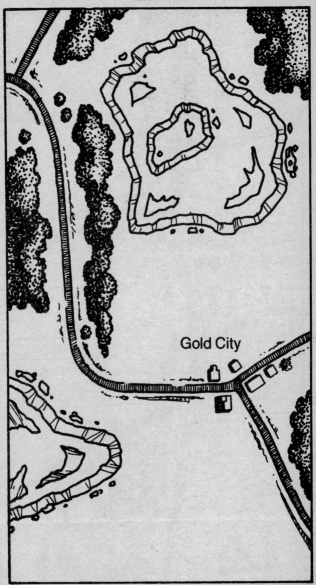

MAP 4

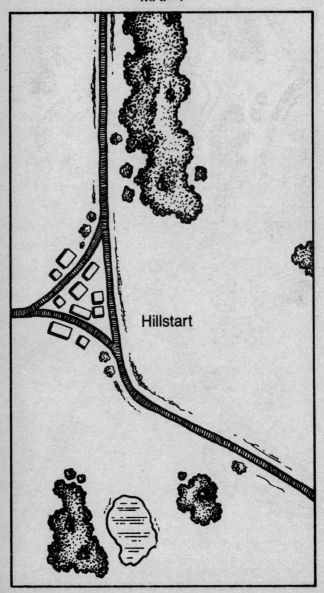

Hillstart

MAP 5

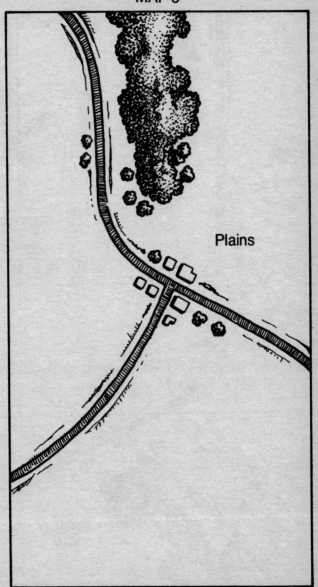

Plains

MAP 6

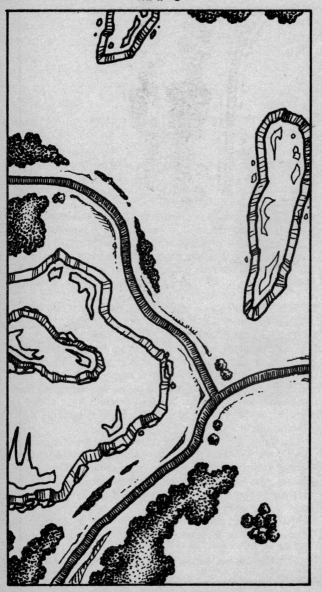

AFTERWORD
by David Drake

I got a very odd feeling from this book when I first read it. It's a rousing action story about soldiers fighting other soldiers with a lot of friendly civilians around to worry about. That's a very real possibility in any war; and almost certainly, if a major war breaks out in Europe, it will be fought initially in West Germany rather than on Warsaw Pact territory.

It's also the environment of the war I saw first-hand, South Viet Nam in 1970, where we were fighting in the territory of our ally in order to save his population from enemies who, by this time, were mostly foreigners from north of the border.

Slammers Down! is about how such a war should be fought. If there's got to be one, this is how I sincerely hope the next war *will* be fought.

And it's very different from the war I saw.

Understand that I don't mean that our troops in Viet Nam were raping and pillaging . . . though I saw some looting, and I have no doubt that there was rape as well. There were 525,000 U.S. servicemen in Nam when I was there, and there was going to be aberrant behavior in-country as surely as there was in the vicinity of Fort Bragg where I did my Basic Training.

The things that concern me in retrospect were matters of governmental policy. Quite frankly, I'd never thought of them in this way until I read the manuscript of the book you hold in your hands. I'm good at compartmentalizing data to keep things that would bother me from doing so. I just hadn't realized *how* good I was at that.

Mad Minutes were accepted doctrine for night-time defense, at least in my unit (the Eleventh Armored Cavalry). The theory was very simple.

Each firebase was surrounded by a berm of earth turned up

by bulldozers. All the fighting vehicles within the firebase faced outward, like spokes around a wheel rim—the tanks; the ACAV's, armored personnel carriers converted into combat vehicles by gunshields around a pair of 7.62mm machine guns and a cupola for the big cal fifty; and other odds and sods on one chassis or the other, bridge tanks and flame tracks and combat engineer vehicles.

At a prearranged time, on radioed orders from the Tactical Operations Center in the middle of the firebase, each vehicle would fire a gun of a single specified caliber out into the night—for one minute.

You can't see a hell of a lot during the Vietnamese night, but there wasn't much background noise. The theory was that if the enemy were assembling at the treeline to attack us, the sudden blast of fire would startle some of them into shooting back before they were ready. Because all the U.S. fire came from weapons of one type, the distinctly different sound of the hostile weapon would warn everyone in the firebase instantly.

I've never even heard of an instance where a Mad Minute forestalled an NVA attack, but that may have happened somewhere, sometime. What certainly did happen was that we put a lot of ordnance into very peaceful countryside occupied by the people we were over there to protect.

Sure, part of the time we were in a region of Cambodia which was, by decree of President Nixon, wholly controlled by the enemy; and part of the time we were in War Zone C, again defined as a free-fire zone in which anything living was fair game.

But often we were laagered in areas as settled and peaceful as any in Viet Nam. We were about twenty miles northwest of Saigon the time the resupply helicopters brought several loads of the widely hated Dial-A-Dink rounds for the 90mm main guns of the tanks. For the next several nights the squadron fired the stuff off during Mad Minutes to get rid of it.

Dial-a-Dink rounds were true shrapnel shells (as opposed to canister rounds which were big shotgun shells whose charge of steel pellets came out of the muzzle loose). A Dial-A-Dink shell casing looked like that of an ordinary high explosive shell. Inside the casing was material that would fragment—notched piano wire like modern grenades, as I remember—when the bursting charge in the shell's core went off.

The shell's nose fuse had a rotating dial that could be set to detonate at a chosen range beyond the muzzle (thus Dial-A-Dink). The theory was that the gunner would determine the range of hostile infantry and report it to the loader, who would set the fuse for that range. The shell would be aimed to burst in the air over the infantry, doing much more damage than mere high explosive fired into the ground near the target.

If you doubt that anybody I knew spent that kind of time fucking around in a firefight, you've got better sense than anybody in the Pentagon seemed to. Besides, the fuses were notoriously unreliable: some went off early, some didn't go off at all. This isn't a comment on the workmanship of what I was told was a very expensive piece of ordnance. The fuses, like the shells around them, were accelerated from zero to several thousand feet per second in a microsecond. *Nothing* can be expected to work perfectly after treatment like that.

So the squadron commander called a lot of 90mm Mad Minutes to get rid of the damned stuff.

The tank main guns were really impressive to be around when they were firing. By 1970 the nineties were obsolete for tank-versus-tank combat, but they were nonetheless more powerful than the German eighty-eights which ruled all the battlefields on which they appeared during World War II. Their range in direct fire was several miles, and each shell weighed about twenty pounds.

My first experience with nineties firing came during an unexpected Mad Minute in Cambodia. I was standing at the piss tube behind our tent, roughly between two tanks. They were fifty feet or so apart.

They fired simultaneously, and I thought the world had ended. The night flashed green—copper vaporizing from the rotating bands of the shells—and a hammer hit me on either side of the head. I remember screaming, but one of the tanks had gotten off a second round before I had enough composure to cover my ears.

That was what it was like when the ninety was shooting away from you. I don't know how it was felt to be downrange from them when they fired; but the civilians in the three nearby villages certainly learned during the week we were laagered there.

I saw B-52 raids and napalm runs. Every night our artillery would fire Harassment and Interdiction missions out into the darkness; some of the bomblets from their firecracker rounds would lie in the target area the next morning, unexploded until some boy herding his buffalo stepped on one. I could tell you about automatic ambushes, directional mines fired by tripwires laid across the paths between villages. . . .

But the casualness of Mad Minutes says about all you need to know about the way America conducted war in Viet Nam.

And because it was something *I* did without even thinking about it, it says more than I needed to remember about myself.

—David Drake

ABOUT THE AUTHOR

Todd Johnson served as a scout with the 1st Infantry Division Forward in Germany for four years, leaving the service as a sergeant. Mr. Johnson professes a lifelong interest in military science, and military games in particular. He was the principal designer for Mayfair Games' *The Worlds of Boris Vallejo Game*, and consultant for several others.

When not writing books, Mr. Johnson is a computer programmer with great interest in flying and the space industry. He now lives in California, after having spent fifteen years in Ireland. This is Mr. Johnson's first book.